Magne Sandnes

About the Author

GUNNHILD ØYEHAUG is an award-winning Norwegian poet, essayist, and fiction writer. Her novel *Wait, Blink* was made into the acclaimed film *Women in Over-sized Men's Shirts*. She has also worked as a coeditor of the literary journals *Vagant* and *Kraftsentrum*. Øyehaug lives in Bergen, where she teaches creative writing.

About the Translator

KARI DICKSON was born in Edinburgh, Scotland, and grew up bilingual. She has a BA in Scandinavian studies and an MA in translation. Before becoming a translator, she worked in theatre in London and Oslo. She currently teaches in the Scandinavian department at the University of Edinburgh.

ADDITIONAL PRAISE FOR *KNOTS*

"From my first reading of *Knots* in the original Nynorsk, I have been captivated by Gunnhild Øyehaug's wit, imagination, ironic social commentary, and fearless embrace of any and every form of storytelling. These are stories to be relished, inspiring in their art and humanity both. How fortunate that we can now read them in Kari Dickson's sparkling and magically faithful English."

—Lydia Davis, author of *Can't and Won't*

"The rich variety of the stories in *Knots* contributes to the sense of unpredictability and wonder that pervades the book. But wonder in *Knots* doesn't spring from variety alone. It arises from Gunnhild Øyehaug's very conception of story, and only a rare writer is capable of such sustained surprise."

—Stuart Dybek, author of *Ecstatic Cahoots*

"Her work is playful, often surreal, intellectually rigorous, and brief. She sometimes resembles Lydia Davis. . . . Like Davis, she moves easily from the theoretical to the humanely engaged . . . and, like Davis, she can produce stabs of emotion, unexpected ghost notes of feeling, from pieces so short and offbeat that they seem at first like aborted arias. . . . Øyehaug is intensely interested in consciousness and in the pictures consciousness makes; this emphasis constantly humanizes her experiments in abstraction and the fantastical."

—James Wood, *The New Yorker*

"Øyehaug's newly translated collection charts entanglements of all kinds, from difficult families and first loves to more metaphysical experiments that combine a crisp minimalism with endearingly offbeat conceits. . . . [Øyehaug's] stories are as original as they are joyously delicate and tranquil."

—*Publishers Weekly*

"Formally playful, poignant, understated, and often acutely funny, Øyehaug's English-language debut teems with humanity. . . . A near-perfect collection about the knots we tie ourselves into and the countless ways we intertwine in the pursuit of sex, love, compassion, and family."

—*Kirkus Reviews* (starred review)

"Replete with IKEA crises, uncuttable umbilical cords, and lewd eulogies, these stories will have you laughing at the strange way the 'world has organized today for you.'"

—*O, The Oprah Magazine*

KNOTS

Stories

GUNNHILD ØYEHAUG

Translated from the Norwegian by Kari Dickson

Picador   Farrar, Straus and Giroux   New York

This translation has been published with the financial support of NORLA.

picadorusa.com • instagram.com/picador
twitter.com/picadorusa • facebook.com/picadorusa

Picador® is a U.S. registered trademark and is used by Macmillan Publishing Group, LLC, under license from Pan Books Limited.

For book club information, please visit facebook.com/picadorbookclub or email marketing@picadorusa.com.

Designed by Jonathan D. Lippincott

The Library of Congress has cataloged the Farrar, Straus and Giroux edition as follows:

Names: Øyehaug, Gunnhild, 1975– author. | Dickson, Kari, translator.
Title: Knots : stories / Gunnhild Øyehaug ; translated from the
    Norwegian by Kari Dickson.
Description: First American edition. | New York : Farrar, Straus and
    Giroux, 2017.
Identifiers: LCCN 2016045040 | ISBN 9780374181673 (hardcover) |
    ISBN 9780374714994 (ebook)
Subjects: LCSH: Øyehaug, Gunnhild, 1975– —Translations into English |
    BISAC: FICTION / Literary. | FICTION / Short Stories (single author).
Classification: LCC PT8952.25.Y44 A2 2017 | DDC 839.823'8—dc23
LC record available at https://lccn.loc.gov/2016045040

Picador Paperback ISBN 978-1-250-18244-9

Our books may be purchased in bulk for promotional, educational, or business use. Please contact your local bookseller or the Macmillan Corporate and Premium Sales Department at 1-800-221-7945, extension 5442, or by email at MacmillanSpecialMarkets@macmillan.com.

Originally published in Norway by Kolon Forlag as *Knutar*+

First English translation published in the United States by Farrar, Straus and Giroux

First Picador Edition: July 2018

10 9 8 7 6 5 4 3 2 1

One of two things: either the spiral
or to be sent out into the air.
—Christophe Tarkos

Contents

KNOTS

Nice and Mild

This is going to be—no, I don't want to be cate-gorical—this *could* be the start of a virtuous circle. My psychologist has told me that I need to say positive things to myself, only I don't want to be too positive, as that might just make things worse. But I can say this: My life is a mess and I'm going to try to sort it out, starting with the small things. Then, later, I'll be able to deal with bigger, more complicated things; buying blinds is a lifeline that's been thrown to me from dry land as I flail and flounder in the waves, I muse, and park the car outside IKEA.

—

I'm going to buy blinds for my son. He's been com-plaining about it for over six months now, the fact that he doesn't have blinds, so the sun shines straight onto his computer screen. And now I'm going to sort it out. I've been saying for the past six months that I'll buy blinds, and every time my wife's said to me, I can do it, if you like, I've said, No, I will sort it out. And now I'm going to do it. It's a nice, mild autumn day and I'm trying to hold on to that, a simple thought; that it's nice and mild. At home, the DVR is recording the match between Anna Kournikova and Serena Williams, I try to hold on to that: the very fact that I'm recording the match and not watching it live is the start of the virtuous circle that buying the blinds was going to start, and what's more, I've come here on my own and no one—that's to say, my wife—knows that I'm here. I didn't say anything about what I was going to do, I didn't even say I was going out; she was in the garden no doubt in her windproof jacket raking the leaves, so I ran out. I want to surprise her in the same way that I'm going to surprise myself. She won't know anything about it, she'll just go into our son's room and see the blinds hanging there and realize that I am starting to sort things out. I don't reflect at all on the fact that I'm basically sneaking off to sort things out, and don't see it as clearly contradictory. It shows initiative. I'm showing myself that all is not lost, which will have positive consequences over time. At home, Anna Kournikova is hitting tennis balls over a net, and I'm not there to watch it, I'm here, and I've been driving around the parking lot for a while now trying to find a space near the perimeter, and I've managed; several times I've felt small waves of claustrophobia and thought, I have to get away from here, before it's too late, before the cars, the people, and the buildings are on top of me and smother me, until my heart explodes with a whistling nothing, but I've weathered the storm, I've talked to myself, said simple things like: *I'm going to buy blinds. My life is a mess and I want to try to sort it out, starting with the small things.* I repeat: *I'm going to buy blinds.* Remind myself that everything will be normal, everything will be fine. I will sort it out. I'm going to go in, find the blinds, pay, and leave. At home, Anna Kournikova is hitting tennis balls over a net. And I am not there to watch. I am here, I open the car door, get out, it's nice and mild, close the car door, try not to make an ironic face because I'm thinking such simple, positive things, I try not to see myself from the outside, I try not to think, Idiot, idiot, get away from here, can't you see that being here and thinking positive thoughts is just building up to an enormous anticlimax, it's so obvious, you have to get away, it's going to happen, get out of here, and don't try to pretend that you'll preempt the anticlimax by saying it will happen and thereby prevent it from happening, there's no escape from the way the world has organized today for you. On my way across the parking lot, which I scan nervously from behind dark glasses, trying to ignore the fact that it's full, I think about Anna

Kournikova, Anna Kournikova in a short blue dress, her strong thighs, the grunt as her racket hits the hard yellow ball and sends it over the net to the other side, her face, the concentration, the hot red sand she's standing on, or is it a grass court? Be just as concentrated, just as determined, a single-minded bugger: straight in, straight to the blinds, straight out. *The ball*, I think. I'm almost moved by the thought.

—

Because you never know how things might turn out, you never know how anything will turn out, tomorrow all the walls might fall down, the room disappear, tomorrow you might have gone to pieces, not managed to keep things together, you might stand there looking at your wife in her windproof jacket out in the garden on a day when everything about her is so faint that you can see right through her. If she's standing in the garden in front of the pear tree in her windproof jacket, all you can see is the pear tree. The knotted trunk. The twisted branches. The clustering leaves. A small dog that runs across the field behind the tree, and a magpie that takes flight. She raises her hand to wave, but you don't see her, and move away from the window, withdraw into the room.

—

The doors to IKEA slide open, you go in. Try to focus. You're in IKEA and head upstairs. You just have to concentrate on simple tasks, that you're here to buy blinds, that you're walking up the stairs. I always lose any perception of depth when I'm wearing sunglasses, which makes things difficult on stairs, so I take them off and try to put them in the breast pocket of my denim jacket, but miss and they just kind of slide down the front of my jacket, shit, I have to pay attention to what I'm doing, I look down at the breast pocket as my hand guides the sunglasses toward the pocket, then I trip, I trip on the stairs and fall in a very inelegant way just as two teenage girls pass me and giggle because I, an old man, have tripped and am lying sprawled out on the stairs. Don't take it as a sign, don't think NOW EVERYTHING HAS FALLEN, get up. Stand still for a moment, don't rush on as though you were embarrassed and trying to get away in the hope that no one saw you, take your fall with composure and dignity and almost make a point of it by standing there polishing your glasses, which of course, OF COURSE, are now scratched. You've fallen and you know it, and it doesn't matter, except that it hurt, naturally (demonstrate this by touching your knee and making a face and whistling through your teeth). You can stand there a while longer, maybe smile wryly to yourself, then you can start to climb the stairs slowly, while you think that never has Henri Bergson's theory of laughter been better demonstrated, no, it was Baudelaire, of course, Baudelaire's theory of laughter, which is based on the idea (and you have to show that you're thinking, that the fall has given you a certain insight, by looking up slightly to the side and smiling to yourself, maybe smile and look down the stairs, maybe nod, once up and down, but that might perhaps be a bit much) that it is never the one who slips and falls on the street who laughs, but the person walking by who sees it, *unless*, Baudelaire says, the person who falls is a philosopher and able to reflect on his fall, able to see himself from the outside. You laugh a little. You reflect on your fall, and laugh a little. *That*, I think as I grimace to myself in a mirror that is suddenly there, *is how you should take a fall on the stairs at IKEA, you pathetic bloody idiot.* My knee is throbbing. My heart is thumping. I stop at the top of the stairs, put my sunglasses in my pocket.

—

There are so many people at IKEA today, why did I come here on a day when there are so many people? I feel naked without my sunglasses, I try putting them on again, but it's too silly, and in any case, it's difficult to see anything with them on indoors, they make you trip and they're scratched, it looks ridiculous, I put them in the breast pocket of my denim jacket, fuck that I should fall, my knee hurts a bit, but I try not to limp. I try not to limp through the numerous kitchen, living room, and bedroom interiors and then I suddenly spot the neighbors, they're standing discussing a couple of transparent salad bowls, and I almost run and hide behind the poster display racks. You have to pass through that section to get to the blinds, and I look through the posters while I wait for them not to notice me, to decide whether or not to take the salad bowls and move on, I go through sunsets and Monet's water lilies, and the thought that I'm standing here hiding makes me want to scream, today when you wanted to sort everything out and breathe, to start the virtuous circle that has already started by recording Anna Kournikova on the DVR, you have to stop hiding here behind the posters, you have to go and find the damn blinds, you have to say hello to the neighbors, say that you think the salad bowls are very nice, say everything is fine when they ask how things are, and then carry on. I take a deep breath, step out; the neighbors have moved on. I put on my sunglasses. At home, Anna Kournikova is belting yellow balls over the net. At home, my wife is out in the garden or wherever she's standing in her windproof jacket, crying because she thinks that I can't breathe. At home, my wife is standing looking down at her hands, which are so helplessly pale, she closes her eyes, pulls her hair back tight from her temples, to stop herself from crying because she thinks that I can't breathe, that she is smothering me, which is why I can't face doing anything, why I sit on the sofa for most of the day and watch TV and feel that I'm turning into an old man and that life, in short, is over. She's found an old photo of us, put it in a frame on the mantelpiece, quite casually. As if she suddenly had a frame to spare and needed a picture and just happened to find this one. It's a good picture. She's looking down with a shy smile, and I'm looking straight at her, and it's easy to see that I love her. Our heads are in sync in the photograph, we seem to be leaning gently toward each other, if you just saw the outline of our heads, they might look like two mountain ridges feeding into each other and there's a nice, mild light around our hair. NO, IT'S NOT THAT I CAN'T BREATHE! But now I'm going to sort it out, and she won't know anything about it, she'll just go into the room and see the blinds hanging there. I'll sort that out first, and then the rest. I'm going to get blinds for my son, that's what I'm going to get. The sunlight floods into his room through the window, unhindered, hits the computer screen and makes it hard for him to see. And now I'm going to sort it out.

—

Unbelievable: my wife is standing over there by the blinds. I'm walking through the glassware and cutlery and salad bowls when I see my wife standing over by the blinds together with the neighbors and an IKEA employee. She's standing by the blinds. At home, Anna Kournikova is standing in a short blue dress hitting yellow tennis balls over the net. Her thighs are powerful and brown. At home, the DVR is whirring in the living room, and the rake is leaning against the pear tree, or the side of the house, or somewhere else. No one is standing pulling her hair back from her temples and no one is sitting apathetically watching TV. I'm wearing my scratched sunglasses and I'm in IKEA looking at my wife, who has got there before me, and I'm wondering how on earth I can get away without her seeing me, I should go over and say "long time no see"—or something funny like that, but I'm embarrassed. I should have done this six months ago. And now I was going to sort it out. I look at her, and hesitate as I look at her. She looks so different standing here in her own life for a moment, there's something about the way she looks at the IKEA employee, something in her face, or perhaps more something about her cheeks, that says she doesn't know anything about blinds, that she trusts him implicitly, but that she doesn't know if she's given him the right information, she's no doubt forgotten to check how wide the window is, and I can see her discussing it with the neighbors, because they have exactly the same windows as us, they point to one of the blinds, and I stare, I stare at her cheeks that look so naked. She's so beautiful. And then, when she notices me, as I'm more or less reversing, without realizing that that's what I'm doing, as quietly as I can, into a table of see-through salad bowls, and the salad bowls just keep falling and falling, she just smiles. She actually smiles.

Taking Off, Landing

Things weren't so bad! Geir had his van, he had a sign on the roof that read "Eggs and Prawns." He didn't have many eggs and prawns in the car, but he had a place at the market, and the market was by the harbor, so he could just sit there. Day in and day out. Watch the seagulls taking off and landing, landing and taking off. Reminisce about his own time at sea. Watch the people passing by, carrying their heavy shopping bags, slipping on the ice. Today he had laughed a lot, thanks to a particular spot outside the flower shop, where no fewer than three people had fallen on their asses in a row.

—

Things were good. There was so much to see. So even though he didn't exactly have a lot to do, it was far from boring sitting in his van all day, in the same place. And it wasn't cold. He had his thermal overalls on and a trapper's hat. And he could listen to the radio. And then that oddball Asle came along carrying a rather large stone. It looked like he was struggling; the poor guy probably didn't have much strength, thin and weedy as he was. What was he going to do with the stone?*

Jump? Geir had to laugh.

But poor Asle. It was something to do with him not getting enough oxygen to the brain, because he'd

---

*Dive

Brilliant explanation: When Asle was small, he lived at the top of Syrup Hill. Every morning when he went to school, he got sticky with syrup right up to his thighs, and every afternoon when he went home from school, he got sticky right up to his thighs all over again. Walking home was hardest; he had to use every ounce of strength in his little body to get his legs to move through the thick syrup. He was often late for supper and his mother got annoyed as a result and he didn't get anything to eat until late in the evening, after she'd sat in the living room knitting and cooled down as she watched the lights from the houses below rise up to meet the dark that was falling, glittering like melted sugar. Eventually, she got up with a sigh, peeled a couple of cold potatoes, cut them into pieces, put them in the gravy, sliced the meatballs and carrots in two, warmed everything up on the wood-burning stove that stood crackling and spitting by the wall, then went into his room, where he lay crying with hunger. "Supper" was all she said, and Asle jumped up from the bed, ran out to the kitchen, gobbled down the food. He often had a sore tummy afterward. His mother stroked his hair and took his sticky trousers. Threw them into a big bowl of steaming water. "Do you have to get so sticky every time?" she shouted from the bathroom, but he was prepared and had stuffed pieces of cold potato in his ears. He went into the living room with the pieces of potato in his ears, looked out at the lights glittering in all the houses, there was a dull humming in his ears like when he dived underwater in summer, and as he stood there looking out over the houses that lay shining like treasure on the seabed, he was suddenly struck by such a strong desire to be underwater that it brought tears to his eyes. He wanted to take a stone, a big stone, in his hands and jump so he was sure to go all the way to the bottom.

been blowing glass for so long. He'd blown some incredible things. But in the end, he could only blow glass bubbles. Which made Geir laugh. And he hung them up in the trees! There was a tap at the window; he wound it down. It was Åsta. "Oh, is it you, Åsta?" he said, and Åsta looked at him sternly from under her red hat. It was a round, woolly hat, the red fuzz waving gently. "I see you've got a sea anemone on your head today," he said, and Åsta pursed her lips. "Oh, hush, will you," she said, and pushed her shopping cart demonstratively into the car door. "Have you got any eggs and prawns?" He turned toward the backseat as if to look, then leaned forward again. "Looks like it's empty, sorry." "Well, isn't that a surprise," Åsta said. "And yet you've still got a place at the market," she said. "You'll have to come back tomorrow," he said. "I'll have a new supply then." "That'd be something, wouldn't it," Åsta said, and took hold of the cart. He rolled up the window just as she was saying something, smiled and nodded to her as she sent him an indignant look before tottering gingerly off down the road on her ice grips.

—

Geir looked around. There were very few people out and about at this time of morning. It must be the slippery ice that was deterring them from taking their normal walks. He grabbed a bar of chocolate that was on the seat beside him, and just then, out of the corner of his eye, he saw Asle standing behind the factory wall at the start of the old, rotten quay; he took a few steps out onto the rotten wood. Geir leaned toward the windshield so he could see better. What was he doing there? He rolled down the window to shout that it wasn't safe, that the quay was rotten, that he mustn't go any farther, but just then Asle took a couple of peculiar, heavy steps, then gathered himself and jumped. A huge splash. Geir swallowed. A chill washed through him. He looked at the backseat. At the chocolate in his hand. Gripped the steering wheel, leaned toward the windshield. He was a little bewildered now.

Small Knot

Kåre came into this world with an umbilical cord that no one could cut. The umbilical cord was attached to a placenta that refused to come out. It stayed where it was; it wouldn't budge. They couldn't cut the umbilical cord, or remove the placenta. "This is a bit of a quandary," the doctor said. *A bit.* At first, his father took it as a personal defeat, the fact that he couldn't cut the umbilical cord: he thought he must be the lowest of the low, a wretch of a father, when he couldn't even do a simple thing like that. To be fair, the umbilical cord was both thick and slippery, but it wasn't abnormally thick. Just abnormally strong. And there was comfort for Kåre's father in the fact that no one else could cut it, none of the nurses, none of the doctors, no matter how hard they tried. "We'll have to find a way to live with it, Marianne," Kåre's father said. "You're attached for life, no doubt about it."

Marianne didn't really have any objection. In many ways, it was easier to keep an eye on the little boy, and she could just pull in the cord if she lost sight of him, or he ran away and hid. Having a private life with his father was of course problematic, but they managed all the same: it was just a matter of doing it as quietly as possible, with as little movement as possible. Kåre's father, on the other hand, found it harder and harder to cope with the situation, he *needed* movement! he would sometimes shout when he got really angry, often after some public outing: a shopping trip or a walk in the park, when people had stared at the grayish white, naked cord between the mother and son. And at Kåre's father, so he believed, as he walked half a step behind them with his head bowed. He couldn't stand it any longer. He left.

—

Marianne didn't really have any objection. In many ways, it was easier to live the way they had to live, when she could concentrate on keeping up with her son. There was so much she had to do. She had to run everywhere, climb trees, jump in hay, ride a bike, play football, go to his friends' houses. And all the time she tried to be invisible, didn't want to hinder her son's development, knew that she had to let him do things, try things, she didn't want to be a ball and chain, so when they were out being naughty and getting up to mischief, she closed her eyes. Stood outside the bathroom when they smeared it with toothpaste. Hid behind a tree when they secretly smoked a cigarette in the ditch. And covered her eyes when she had to go into the changing room with Kåre before and after swimming. And during Kåre's sexual debut, as a drunk fourteen-year-old at a party, she lay hidden as best she could under the bed and covered her ears.

—

When Kåre got married, Marianne naturally moved in with the young couple. They made a bedroom for her next to their own, because the bride couldn't cope with Marianne sleeping in the same room, so that's what they did. It was actually nothing more than a dividing wall with a small opening so they could feed the cord through before they all went to bed. But the bride thought she saw Marianne's eye staring at them through the crack. Marianne said it wasn't true, but the bride was adamant, and made a curtain that she hung in front of the opening. The curtain was obstructed by the umbilical cord and the bride wailed and collapsed on the floor. "She's everywhere!" she sobbed. "She's everywhere, Kåre, and nothing works, I can't bear it! I can't bear it!" she cried, and in her desperation she bit the umbilical cord with all her might. "Ow!"

Kåre and Marianne screamed, then looked at each other, horrified, through the opening; they didn't know that the cord had become sensitive. The bride just sobbed. "I'm leaving," she said. "I'm le-e-e-aving." And she left.

—

Kåre didn't really have any objection. In many ways it was much easier to live the way they had to live; now that his mother was getting old, he would have to start taking her slowing pace into consideration. He could no longer do the things he wanted to do: he couldn't go out with his friends—she got tired so quickly, but it wasn't that, she could happily sit in the pub and sleep, she said, but he didn't want to, he said, he didn't need to anymore. The truth was that he'd always been embarrassed when she fell asleep; her chin dropped onto her chest and she dribbled out of the corner of her mouth. So he would just have to manage without. "It's always been you who's done what I want, Mom," he said. "Now I can do what you want." So he went with her to play bingo. To the shops. And when she fell asleep in public places, he didn't feel so embarrassed anymore, he even felt affection for her, as she sat there with a thin thread of spittle hanging from her chin; she was his mother. And she had gone with him everywhere. He loved her. He eventually got used to a quiet life, to a few hours with the crossword and knitting, to longer and longer afternoon naps, to all sorts of TV series and radio programs. To shuffling in his slippers across the linoleum. To going to bed at nine. It was peaceful. Pleasant.

—

But one day, in the middle of breakfast, Marianne died. Her heart had stopped, the doctors said, and Kåre was inconsolable. They also said that now that she was dead, they *had* to cut the umbilical cord. Because if not, Kåre would have to move to the graveyard. "But the cord's sensitive now," Kåre said. "It'll hurt!" "Have you never heard of anesthetic?" they asked, and Kåre blushed. Of course he had, he mumbled. So they gave Kåre a general anesthetic. They were going to try to separate Kåre from his dead mother. But nothing worked. "What the hell," the doctors said. "This is unbelievable!" The placenta had shriveled into a lump the size of a raisin that was attached to her pelvic bone; it had become part of the skeleton. Not even the part of the umbilical cord that was turning green could be cut by scissors, knives, or laser. Nothing worked. The bond was not to be broken. "Kåre, we have to cut loose part of her skeleton if you're to be freed," they said. Kåre looked at them, as if he was frightened they were going to hit him. His

eyes wide open, his ears flat against his head like a
dog; the specialist whispered he would live like a dog,
when Kåre cried: "No, it's fine, don't do it!" "Then
we'll have to tie a small knot in it, to stop her death
from feeding into you. There's nothing more we can
do, Kåre, we're terribly sorry," the doctors said.
Kåre said it was fine. He just asked them to request
that the funeral directors make a hole in the coffin,
so the umbilical cord could get through. And to apply
to the local council for permission to build in the
graveyard.

—

Permission was granted, but the house could not be
higher than the highest gravestone, or wider than was
possible without disturbing the other graves, but that
was fine for Kåre, he didn't have much room to ma-
neuver in any case, now that the umbilical cord had
been shortened by six feet. It was fine, he had got used
to the quiet life and he passed the days as he had before his mother died, doing the crossword, watching
TV, listening to the radio. He shuffled his slippers
against the wall every now and then, looked out of the
window at the various funeral parties that passed once
a week. To see if he could see her. She was always
part of the funeral party, but never seemed to know

any of the others standing there crying and comforting each other. She always stood on the periphery, dressed in black, her small white face looking down at the ground.

—

He had noticed her the very first time he saw a funeral party from his new home; she'd been right at the back and tripped on her long skirt, which was even longer thanks to the rain. One day when there was a lot of wind and rain, she had tripped right outside his house. It was well situated that way, he thought, it was just by the small gravel path that wound through the graveyard, so that funeral parties had to walk past to get to the graves. And when she stood up again and brushed down her knees, she looked straight at him. Heaven and earth stood still. And then she moved on. He watched her go. She folded her arms across her chest; she was a thin, dark line at the back of the party, in a far too long and wet skirt. He thought that he would love to kiss her in the wild wind. And the kiss would be like long hair in the wind, or like long grass in the wind, it would both suck them down to the ground and tug at them, as if trying to blow them away.

—

Oh!

—

He waited for her every day. She had started to look in now, every time she passed, they'd started to acknowledge each other, only just, with their eyes, but there was something, he didn't know what it was, a kind of understanding, and then one day he dared, he had written a small message and held it up to the window, in the hope she would see: COME HERE, it read. Come here. He had tidied as best he could, washed the floor, picked a few flowers from his mother's grave and put them on the tiny table, and he thought that everything looked nice. The only thing that made him a little uneasy was the umbilical cord: his part up to the knot was gray and healthy and fine, but Marianne's side got blacker and blacker, closer and closer to the small knot, and he didn't know if the knot was strong enough to keep her death at bay. And he had no idea what the girl whose name he didn't know would think. He was standing there with flour on his hands when there was a knock at the door. He'd thought of trying to powder Marianne's end of the umbilical cord, but now just wiped his hands as quickly as he could on a tea towel and opened the door. It was her. There she stood, small and dark, with her pale, pale face. Her arms folded across her chest. "Come in," he said, smiling. "Come in."

⸺

She had no family, she told him, and she was so lonely! She was utterly alone in the world! She cried in his lap. Funerals were the only place she dared to go to meet people, people were so open at funerals, they wept and opened up, and even if people didn't know her, they assumed that she had known the deceased in some way or another, that perhaps she had done little jobs for them, cut their hair or something. Because they welcomed her, gave her coffee at the reception afterward, talked to her, asked how she had known the deceased, and generally she said something nice, something she'd heard during the service, and they asked about her, who she was, what she did. He stroked her hair. "But now you can come here," he said. "For as long as I've got left." "What do you mean?" she asked. "You see the cord that comes out from my belly?" he asked. She lifted her head and wiped the tears from her eyes. "Yes! What *is* it?"

⸺

He told her everything.

—

"She just *left*?" she said, when he told the bit about his bride. "Yes," Kåre said, and felt a lump in his throat. Something was being squeezed somewhere. It stung and stung. "So you've got no children," she said. He shook his head. "Nor have I. And I so want one! I want something that is mine! A home! Someone to be at home with!" She looked at him. "Do you think . . . would you want me, I mean, in theory, am I something worth having, am I something that someone would want—to be blunt, what do you think?" she said. "Would you want *me*?" he asked. "After all, I'm a man bound to his dead mother by an unbreakable umbilical cord!" "I don't want anyone else," she said, and threw her arms around his neck. Her body was so small and he could feel her vibrating. Kåre was trembling. "Who knows what my genes might produce," he said. "You might get a child with an umbilical cord like mine." "I don't want anything else!" she cried with joy. And now he *was* going to kiss her.

Gold Pattern

The sound of the wind rustling through the grass and aspen trees around the yard at her grandma's house can be heard through the open window. But she's straddled him on a wooden chair in the narrow kitchen and barely notices the wind. They cycled out to the small house that's not been lived in since her grandma died, they giggled up the steps, then she hitched up her skirt and planted her feet on the stretchers between the chair legs on either side. She's standing on the balls of her feet, one hand on the door handle, the other on the kitchen table, lifting herself up and down. He's holding her buttocks and helping, looking red and pained as he bangs the back of his head against the yellow-paneled wall. They met at a party six months ago, and as they stood on opposite sides of the room and looked at each other, they just knew, they said when they were lying on a mattress on her floor a few hours later, stroking each other's hair, that this had to happen. They lay like this at regular intervals over a three-week period, until she'd had enough because she thought she detected a trace of reluctance to commit on his part. It upset her. "Don't talk to me again," she said. They're not talking to each other now. She feels her thighs burning and he is deep into a brain-draining darkness.

—

They met again at a party three months ago, and as they stood there on either side of the room looking at each other, they just knew, they said when they were lying together on a mattress on the floor in her room later, they just knew that this had to happen. And it happened at regular intervals over a three-week period until she couldn't take anymore because she detected a trace of reluctance to commit on his part. And he didn't run his hands through her hair anymore. He held her by the hips and banged his head against her stomach and said: "I don't want to upset you. But I can't have a girlfriend right now. It's just not the right time."

—

They met again three weeks ago, at the Shell station in the middle of the night, and as they stood there on either side of the freezer and a stand of sunglasses, they just knew, they said when they were lying on a mattress on the floor in her room later, they just knew that this had to happen. He slides his hands up to her breasts, which move up and down under her top, and his eyes look as though they're sinking back into his head behind his eyelids, like two heavy stones. The kitchen window is ajar, the stay rattles, the panes vibrate in the wind that blows over the fields of tall grass, through the leaves of the aspen trees outside, and makes the rope on the flagpole slap against the pole in a hollow metal rhythm. She thinks: This, the fact that we're here having sex now, must mean that he's changed his mind.

—

A cat meows in the wind, but he doesn't hear, he moves his hands back down under her buttocks. It's getting closer; he grabs her by the hips. Always, when it's nearly over, he turns her around, holds her by the hips. She, on the other hand, has always hoped that he won't turn her around, but rather come looking at her face-to-face, so she can see what he looks like in that moment. She believes that this expression, this expression of ecstasy, will show her the truth, something that he doesn't want to show her; she thinks that he loves her, secretly, but that he doesn't dare to admit it, not even to himself, but she thinks that his expression in that moment will give him away, will express something like love. She has to see it, she has to know that what she believes is true, is there. It would be enough. And that is what makes her into what one could only call a fool.

—

The wind sings in the grass and soughs through the aspen trees, everything is sighing and whispering, everything is green and comes in waves. They're in the kitchen trembling, and now she feels him letting go of her hips at precisely the moment she sees an old porcelain cup in the sink with a gold pattern that has almost been washed off, she listens, and now she *must*, she will see his face: she turns around. But she lifts herself a little too much and he slips out of her with a sucking sound just before the crucial moment, and all she sees is a red face twisted in frustration before she loses her balance and falls forward onto the floor, onto some rag rugs made of something that resembles plastic. He gets up from the chair, asks if she's all right, hears a yes, and then finishes off against her back, which is arched in front of him, just as somewhere outside in the wind the cat meows loudly and she realizes how tired her thighs are.

Overtures

It's warm, and Ragnhild needs to pee. She's kneeling on her bed, with her elbows on the windowsill, looking out at the birch tree that stretches its branches toward the window, rocking on her heel, which she's sitting on to delay going to the bathroom. As the birch branches wave back and forth in the drowsy wind, she sees through them over the road and up to the field where one of her cousins is lying on a sun lounger with one knee pulled up and her arms slightly out to the side. And she sees one of the boys from next door over by the fence that divides the two properties, lying on the ground peeping in through the planks. He's the cutest boy in the neighborhood, the one everyone's in love with, and her cousin knows that he's lying there, that's why she's pulled up her knee. A girl always looks better with her knee pulled up. Ragnhild's heel is holding in so much pee now that she almost feels sick. But she carries on rocking to keep it in even longer. The toilet sits in the danger zone, a danger zone where creaking doors might burst open and great vacuum cleaner pipes might suck you into the living room and spit you out by the piano. Grandpa has been so looking forward to it, they'll say, and you'll have to sit down on the piano stool, feel the ridged fabric under your thighs, because the thin dress you didn't really want to wear because you think you're too fat for it—but it's still better than shorts—rides up when you sit down; you'll have to look at the music, which you've looked at a hundred times before, and still think it looks illegible and completely unknown, you'll have to feel your heart thumping, the sweat on your fingers, and you'll have to play, on keys that get slippier and slippier. The first line, knowing all the time that you have to play two more pages before you can stand up and take the applause you know you don't deserve because you've made so many mistakes along the way. And you'll get a hug that smells of aftershave and feel the thin shoulders under the thin shirt and say *hmm, hmm, right*, when they say that one day, in a few years' time, you'll make your debut in the concert hall, the Aula, at the University of Oslo, and you know that it's impossible and blatantly not true, and that everyone knows that, that the Aula is just something they say, and you hate it, you hate that hall at the University of Oslo, you want to scream and shout that you hate them all because you have to play the piano for them when you can't and only make mistakes, and it's not

fair to force someone to do something they don't want
to do. And that what they're saying about the Aula
in Oslo is just rubbish. Aaauulaa. It's a big, horrible
word that makes her shudder.

—

She is NOT going to go to the bathroom. She rocks
and rocks. Moves over to the small window next to the
main one, lifts the latch and gently pushes it open with
her finger. Carefully checks the windowsill to make sure
there are no spiders, one of those big black ones that
come out at dusk and stare at her lying on the bed,
reading or dreaming, because she doesn't want to be
out there, where you have to wear shorts, and where
you're always being bothered by wasps and bees and
all kinds of insects, which make it impossible for her
to have the window open at night, so her parents have
to sneak in after she's gone to sleep and open it, because
they can't bear the thought of her sleeping in that
boiling-hot room. It's not healthy, they say, it's not sur-
prising that you get so many headaches in summer,
which sometimes make her howl with rage, and they
don't dare open it again for a few days. Sometimes she
catches them just as they're about to close it again in
the morning, before she's woken up, or so they think,
but she's awake, and she leaps out of bed and shouts:
DID YOU OPEN IT? making them jump as they stand

there in their nighties or underpants, before she forces them to inspect the window and curtains and ceiling for spiders before she can go back to sleep, but more often than not, she lies in bed looking up at the ceiling to see if any of the knots in the wood are in fact moving. Maybe she regrets shouting. Then she'll put on her shorts and go out into the garden for a while and play badminton with her dad. And often there's not as many wasps out there as anticipated. But she doesn't say that. And now she needs to pee so badly she's about to burst. But she keeps rocking, pushing harder against her heel, and then a wasp brushes over her hair and flies into the room, turns abruptly and bashes into the window, making a horrible, flat sound as her hammering heart, which plunged into her pee and squeezed out a few drops as she moved her heel to dodge out of the way, slowly pushes itself back into place in her chest, hammering all the while, and she bolts out of the room and slams the door.

—

When she opens the door a crack thirty seconds later to see if the wasp has flown out, it's banging against the ceiling, like a shark in an aquarium, she thinks to herself. She closes the door. When she opens it a crack again, the wasp is at the window, buzzing up and down in fizzing strips, the sting waiting in its tail. She thinks it's settled. So now she has to decide what to do. She wants to watch what's happening out in the garden. And she doesn't want to play the piano. It's not easy to think straight; she's full to the brim with pee. Light-headed and aching with pee, she puts one leg in front of the other and clenches her thighs together, sits down so she can clench even harder, but doesn't quite manage to hold it in, clings to the door handle, doubles over, twisting and turning: she HAS to pee. Has to go down into the danger zone. Has to tread on the creaky stairs as lightly as possible, tiptoe down the hall, open the door that always jams against the frame and you can't open it without pulling it hard so that when it finally lets go it makes a noise that lets everyone know: someone is going to the bathroom, and it must be Ragnhild, because she's the only one who's not in the living room, where they're sitting drinking coffee because Grandpa has come to see them, and now they'll have to go out and get her to come in and play the piano, because he's been looking forward to it so much. She treads as quietly as she can. Holds on to the banister and tries to step in the places where it creaks least, holds her breath and grits her teeth every time the pee almost bursts out between her legs, which can't be clenched on the stairs. Gets down. Looks to the right; the door to the living room is closed. She hears them laughing; a good thing, as they maybe won't hear her hurrying to the bathroom door, pressing down the handle, trying to open it carefully, carefully, bent over, one foot in front of the other, clenching and clenching, pulling and pulling, but it doesn't help, she *has* to yank, yank; the door makes a loud noise as it opens, she almost leaps into the bathroom, her legs tight together, pulls up her dress, pulls down her underwear, but when she's finally sitting on the toilet her body has forgotten how to pee, what she has to do. And then she closes her eyes.

And pees.

—

But she doesn't flush when she's finished. That would make too much noise. Instead she puts in extra toilet paper, tears the sheets ever so carefully from the roll. Now she has to creep out into the kitchen to get a jam jar, which she can use to catch the wasp, like she's seen her dad do when he doesn't want to kill them; he puts the jam jar over them and then slips a thin piece of paper between the windowpane and the jar opening, lifts the jar slowly away from the window and then holds it out of the open window and pulls away the paper. Then the wasp flies out and you have to close the window quickly before it decides to turn around and fly back in. She pulls up her underwear, pushes open the door, which makes a noise, but not enough for anyone to hear it, she reckons; she steals out into the hall, stands there, listens. No one comes out. By now the boy from next door has probably emerged from his hiding place and said hello, in that nice way that he does.

—

The kitchen door is shut, completely, and it's impossible to open the kitchen door without making a racket. The doors in this house are so old! It annoys her immensely that they don't have new, silent doors, or that no one has at least oiled the hinges so that the old doors they do have creak less. She studies the two doors, the living room door and the kitchen door. She's in a risky midfield position. Either could open at any time. People could come out, get her to come in. And when she opens the kitchen door with the inevitable noise that that entails, one of her parents might already have gone into the kitchen from the living room and they'll be standing there and will force her to go into the living room and sit down at the piano. She tiptoes over to listen at the living room door, and after a while, she's heard all three voices, so can establish that none of them have gone into the kitchen without her noticing. She tiptoes back to the kitchen door. Puts her hand on the handle and then realizes that she still has another door to go, the cupboard door, and that if the kitchen door hasn't already given her away, then the cupboard door certainly will, because it makes a really distinctive sound when it opens. She's lost the battle. And by now her cousin will have smiled her lovely smile and said hello back. Ragnhild opens the door, goes into the kitchen, opens the cupboard door, which makes its distinctive sound; she takes out a medium-sized jam jar, closes the cupboard door, walks out of the kitchen, closes the kitchen door, and runs up the stairs.

Thunders up.

—

She opens the door to her room a crack, nervous that the wasp might now be banging into the doorframe, and that it might fly straight into her face and sting her. But nothing happens. She opens it a little wider, systematically scans the ceiling, the walls, the window; she can't see the wasp anywhere. Nor can she hear any buzzing. She boldly steps into the room, clutching the jam jar to her chest; she ventures farther in, slowly; it's not there. She sits down on the bed, puts the jam jar on the windowsill, and then she sees her cousin and the boy from next door, who is now sitting beside her on the grass and it looks like they're chatting, it looks like they're having a nice time, her eyes get hot, she hates her cousin, she hates the doors in her house, she hates the heat, she hates everything.

She hates the whole world.

There's a knock on the door.

NO, she says.

—

But here she is: the ridged fabric against her thighs because her dress has slid up. The pedals are freezing cold under her bare feet, and the lines of music seem endless. She looks at the first note and can't think where it is on the piano.

—

She thinks her dad understands her confusion, she thinks he's looking at her back, realizes that she has two hands that have no idea where to begin, he hums the first note, just like that, as though he just thought of a note and had to hum it. She thinks, it's an F. F is *there*. F. F

—

She pulls her hands away from the keys, scratches her forehead, leans in toward the music again to show her audience that she has to think about it, ponder, before she can start, that there's a lot to be considered before you can even open with an F. *Hmm*, she says. F.

—

The piano is a closed window. She scratches her forehead. F. F, F, F

—

She gives it a try. But she can hear straightaway that it
wasn't an F. Her dad hums an F again, and now it's no
longer just a coincidence, now it's quite obvious that
that's the note the whole piece starts with and that the
pianist is having problems finding it on the piano.
The pianist concentrates on the keys. Has seen a key
that might *possibly* be the right one. The difficulty now
is to play it so quietly that the pianist, and not the
audience, can hear whether or not it's the right one.
So the pianist has to conceal her hand movements, and
the key, so they can't see it being pressed down. The
pianist has to move forward on the piano stool, accept
that her dress is pulled even farther up her slightly too
fat thighs, that is to say, pull it down with her left hand,
then press her elbows in to her sides, position her right
hand flat over the keys, lean forward so that her back
becomes a screen, and then press, as gently as possible,
the key that might prove to be F.

—

A miracle: it *is* F.

—

So here she is: this is one of Grandpa's favorite pieces, which is basically why she's been practicing it, and when no one is listening, when the house is empty, when all the windows are closed, she plays it well, she can play it by heart, she never wonders where to start, she can play the whole thing with her eyes shut. Can look out into the garden while she's playing, watch the magpies land on the pear tree, then fly off again. But now everything's clouded, there's a tremor in her arm, and she is *not* playing well, she feels quite distinctly like a fat, ugly child who doesn't like the sun, and who can't play the piano, who says *no* and starts over and over again, who hacks her way through Grandpa's favorite piece, and is dreading the final chord, which she knows she can't do and she's almost guaranteed to start crying, but she refuses to do that, she *has* to get it right, and now there's only half a line left, and *here* comes the chord, and it's wrong, it's totally wrong, she has to do it again, she takes a long time to check that her fingers are in the right place, on the right keys, before pressing down.

—

The applause from only three pairs of hands sounds so strange, she turns toward them and smiles gingerly, she's got a lump in her throat, but she swallows it down, smiles with tight lips. "Come here!" Grandpa says, and she gets up from the piano stool and goes over to Grandpa, who has a really proud look on his face, she doesn't understand, he looks so proud, he's smiling, he gives her a hug, she can smell his aftershave, then he holds her firmly by the upper arms and looks into her eyes, still smiling, and she sees that he has tears in his eyes and one is rolling down his cheek, and she's embarrassed, she doesn't know what to do. She laughs a little, and parrots: "Well, it's the University of Oslo concert hall for you next," and they all laugh, and Grandpa hugs her again.

—

Then she's free to go. She goes to her room, but doesn't thunder up the stairs. She's bewildered because she's not angry, but actually quite happy. She looks out of the window. Her cousin is playing badminton with the boy from next door. Her cousin is not very good at badminton, but the boy from next door seems to like that. He laughs, runs after her, throws the cock in her hair, grabs her round the waist, swings her back and forth. Ragnhild wonders what he would say if he found out that *she* is actually very good at badminton, much better than her cousin. She lies down flat on the bed. In a while she'll go down and ask her dad if he wants to play badminton. They won't play in the garden, but rather out on the road below her cousin's house. The boy from next door will see that she can return all the shots that are too far forward and the ones that fly straight into her face. He'll be surprised, he'll stop and stand there watching her and her dad, watch them playing, he'll see that she's awesomely good. He'll see that she's the best. He'll think: I had no idea . . . She's looking forward to it. She almost can't wait.

A Renowned Engineer

Norwegian Essay

When Rimbaud was a little boy, he used to sit at the kitchen table at home in Charleville. He would sit on his chair without moving, his elbows on the table, his chin in his hands, his eyes blank, and stare out of the window. His feet dangling. When he got older, he wrote some of the most disputed poems in world literature, was the lover of someone called Verlaine, was shot in the foot by Verlaine (who was also a poet and used his time in prison after the shooting incident to write some of his finest poems), and traveled to Africa, where he worked as a merchant and an arms dealer for several years. Some say that he worked as a ringmaster in a Stockholm circus. (Others say that he only sold tickets.) Some think he was a slave trader, but I don't believe so. No evidence has been found. He also lived with an Abyssinian woman, but had no children. Nor did he write. He stopped doing that in 1873, after he had written one of the most disputed poems in world literature. He was only nineteen at the time. When anyone in Africa asked him about his writing, he replied disinterestedly: Oh, *that*. Then said nothing more.

—

After many years in Africa, where he traveled a lot, his body was so worn-out that he fell ill; one of his knees swelled up and was sore. There has been much speculation about what kind of pain it was, and what caused it; some people think it was caused by syphilis, others believe he fell off a horse while hunting with the Righas brothers. It has also been said that after he felt that first intense pain in his knee, he rode off furiously on horseback to distance himself from it, but the horse bolted and threw him off in such a way that he hit his sore knee on a tree.

—

Whatever the case, he wrote home to his mother and asked her to send him a long, warm sock that would reach over the knee. The long, warm sock arrived, but didn't help. He had to go back to France. Twelve men carried him out of Africa and onto a ship.

—

The doctor in Marseille could do nothing but amputate. Rimbaud was given a pair of crutches and hoped to return to Africa. But first he wanted to get married. He wanted to marry a fine French girl from a good family; he simply did not understand that he himself, a broken and fevered amputee with very little money, would perhaps not be the first choice for a fine girl from a good family. She might want other things first.

—

Another dream that Rimbaud had before he died soon afterward, as a result of an infection in his amputated leg, or fever, or cancer, was that, once he was married, he would have a child, a son, who would become a renowned engineer, a rich man, who would work in the field of science, a man afraid of nothing, and who would get on in the world and do well in life.

The Girl Holding My Hand

She sees: A park. A pond in the middle of the park. Children running around the pond, playing with small boats on the water. It's late autumn, cold; on the yellowy-brown gravel, adults are sitting in their coats and scarves, with red noses, keeping an eye on what the children are doing. She's drawn by it. She wants to sit on one of the chairs and follow what the children are doing. Then she'll tell me that if she had been the same age as them, or that's to say, as small as them, she would be a child sitting on a chair watching the children. She's afraid. She's afraid of all kinds of things. She would be scared of losing control of the boat. Of bumping into one of the other children's boats. She would be scared of running into one of the other children. And scared of the adults sitting watching. She would be scared that her mom and dad, who were sitting in the chairs in their coats and scarves, would be ashamed of their hopeless child who couldn't con-trol her little boat and kept colliding with the other children. I can see that she's thought about all this, because her eyes are big and sad, and then she turns and looks at the children again. She's hankering. She's longing to sit in the chair and ache. She says something. Let's listen to what she says: "Can't we sit down for a while?" she says. I nod. We find two green chairs and sit down. I look at her and think, almost in wonder, that this is the girl, this is the girl who straddled me and rode me hard on the jangling hotel bed less than an hour ago. That her fair hair had swayed back and forth above me. That she had had no one to bump into then, no boats to lose control of, no parents who thought that their child was hopeless at this, that she should let go of her inhibitions and not be so uptight. I am gripped by love, want to shake her, tell her that she's the most fantastic and uptight and uninhibited person alive. But I know that if I lean over and whisper that in her ear, and that I want to be with her for the rest of my life, that it's very likely that we'll do just that, stay together for the rest of our lives, I know that she won't say anything, her eyes will slip away, but she'll take my hand and squeeze it. That's all. Because she's not in love with me. I know that. I know she's in love with someone else in this town. Obsessed. Someone she tries not to talk about. Someone she tries not to look for on every street corner, in every gallery we go to. Someone we were supposed to meet here by the pond two days ago, but who didn't show up, someone she thinks she sees everywhere—I can feel it in the hand that's holding hers, a faint start, she thinks she sees: a tall guy, with broad shoulders, a thin dark line. An ex. She looks at me: "Shall we go and get something warm to drink? I'm cold," she says. She's done with longing. Or rather: she wants to long a little more, as we leave the pond and she thinks that it's perhaps the last time that we'll pass this place. We stand up, and she takes my hand. Always takes my hand. I can see that she's caught up in something I should not ask about. If I ask about it now, she'll purse her lips and look down at the ground. But I know what it is, know what she's thinking. I know her. She's thinking that this is the last day, and we'll go home without having met him. She's thinking he's somewhere in this town. That it's a long way home. That this was the last chance. That we're not going to pass this way any-more, that it's over now, there's no hope now. I look down at my hand, my hand that's holding hers, think that if I were to squeeze it, the veins would bulge and burst out of her skin—

—

A café appears between the trees. I don't ask her if she wants to go there, I just steer her over and she lets herself be steered. She pretends that everything's fine, that we're heading for a café, that she's going to have to face the counter, an unknown waitress, an unknown place, where she's going to sit down and drink a cup of tea and do it in a way that doesn't give away just how frightened she is. I know what she's going to ask, so I might as well tell her beforehand, before she even opens her mouth, she'll say: "Can you order?" And she'll look at me in the same way that she looked at me as we approached the pond. Those I'm-a-stranger-here-and-frightened eyes. Save-me eyes. She's going to say it now, she slows down so I will be the one who has to put my hand to the door handle and open the door. She stops before I open it and looks at me in the same way that she did when we were at the pond, she says: "Can *you* order?" She's a stranger here, and frightened. Can I save her? I nod, open the door, she looks around. There are grown-ups sitting at the tables, they've taken off their coats and scarves, but they still have red noses. We find an empty table, sit down. It's perfectly clear. He's not here. I see it in her eyes: they dart nervously around the room. It's empty. He's not here.

—

A girl with long dark hair comes over to us with a small notepad, I order. She's got beautiful eyes, and a nice, round backside, I discover as she turns to go and get the tea that I've ordered. She smiled when I tried to order in this language that I don't really speak. The general response is an exasperated shrug. But she smiled. Came back and put the teapot on the table, the two cups, the small metal jug of milk. She smiles at me again. I smile back. I see that the girl sitting beside me sees it too. That I look at her nice, round behind as she walks away. It doesn't stop me. I stare without shame at her mouth when she talks to the old man behind the counter, they kiss each other on the cheek; I stare at her without shame as she puts on her coat, which must have been lying on a chair behind the counter, as she picks up her bag and swings it over her shoulder, without shame as she lifts her hair that has got caught under the collar, she lifts it up at the neck and drops it down her back. Then she walks past us, head held high, smiles at me again, and walks out. Because I don't do it, I don't get up, I don't follow her, I don't catch up with her, don't take her by the hand, I don't pull her into the trees, where there's no one else, I don't stand her up against a tree, I don't kiss her, I don't take my revenge.

—

The tea is strong, I pour in some milk; the thick white jet plunges in and reappears as a wavy pattern. She holds her hands around the cup to warm them. She's thinking about the boats, she's thinking about him.

Her whole face is horribly sad. Just under an hour ago, she was riding me, her fair hair swaying back and forth. Perhaps to make the time pass, saying his name inside.

—

"Shall we go?" I ask. We've finished our tea, he's not here, he's not going to come. I can see that she's impatient. He's out there somewhere. We don't need to drag out the time. We don't need to drag out anything. She gives me a wily smile, as though she's realized what I'm thinking. "Yes, why don't we?" she says, leans over and kisses me. We taste exactly the same, soft, a little bitter. We drag everything out with that kiss. Drag everything out with a couple of soft, sour tongues. We could just as easily call it a day. Draw a line, release ourselves from each other. She takes my face between her hands and looks me earnestly in the eye: "I love you," she says. "And I," I say, brushing her hair back from her temples with both hands, "love you." She takes my hand, and we leave. Our hands are warmer from holding the cups of tea, we drag everything out by leading each other on like this. I just want to laugh. Laugh and laugh and laugh. A small child comes running toward us pulling a green kite, running and running to make the kite fly, the kite bobs up and down in the air behind him. I laugh, without feeling. I feel a dull urge to shake her, shake her out of this, shake me out of this, I take hold of her upper arms listlessly and am about to shake her when we hear a voice behind us; I let go, we turn around at the same time and see the old man from the café coming toward us. "I'm sorry," he says, out of breath, "but you forgot to pay." "Oh," she says, "it wasn't on purpose at all." She finds her wallet in her bag, takes out a note and gives it to him. "Keep the change, please." He thanks her, says it's far too much. She gives him a tight-lipped smile, wants to be friendly. Nods. Puts her wallet back in her bag and takes my hand again. Turns, looks toward the pond. One last time. A slight tremor in her hand. I turn and see that it's him, that it's him she sees. Or someone standing there who looks more like him than anyone else. He stands there, a long, thin line, with broad shoulders, two days too late, his face turned the other way, I can tell that he's smoking, he looks impatient, he doesn't intend to stand here for long. "Hello," I want to shout, my stomach twisting, "hello! Over here." Want to cast her off like a stone. See her spinning round and round in the air. She turns around again, says nothing, holds my hand tight, leads me away. There's a rhythmic crunching on the gravel when the little boy runs past. Some yellowy-brown gravel showers one of my shoes, and I shout a swear word at him that he doesn't understand.

From the Lighthouse

You grew up in a lighthouse that grew out of a tiny rocky island. When you were little, you were only allowed to walk around on the rock if you had a rope around your waist, and when the tide was in, the rock was completely covered by water. If there was a storm, it was impossible to leave the lighthouse, and the only window that could be opened was the small window in the bathroom, and you stood there whenever there was a storm, you stood there with your eyes closed, and felt salt water and finally, finally, fresh air on your face. The only place you had to play was a staircase, a spiral staircase that twisted up through all four floors of the lighthouse; it was your playground, your garden, mountain, valley, and country road. You ran up and down those stairs, ran all the way down to sit on the bottom step, dejected, on evenings when the sea was still and a cruise ship sailed by in the moonlight with music and dancing on the quarterdeck. You stumbled up those same stairs, legs leaden with shame, when you came home one evening after rowing out to the royal yacht to give the crown prince some of the rare shells that only grew on the island where you lived, and the crown prince had been so nice and asked about your schooling, and he was tall and handsome in a blue suit, and the crown princess had stood up on deck and thrown a bar of chocolate down to the crown prince and the crown prince had caught it gracefully, then thrown it down to you in the boat, where you sat in dumb desperation; you couldn't stand up in the boat to curtsy—you had always been given strict instructions that you were not supposed to stand up in a boat, not even for a bar of chocolate from a crown prince, and then the deep blush when you tried to bow instead, but it was impossible, and idiotic, because you were sitting down. It perhaps goes without saying that in situations and surroundings like that, you might long for places where you can stand upright and curtsy, or wander around in any direction, not just up and down. And perhaps it goes without saying that when you then finally, finally get ashore and there are suddenly streets—dry, wide streets and sidewalks bathed in sunlight, and avenues and entire parks with endless grass—that you then lose your balance, feel dizzy and sick and trip up, and it perhaps goes without saying that when the dizziness doesn't subside, and you don't give up, but get up and try again, then stumble and fall, that then and there, it might seem like your balance nerve has permanently fallen out of your body and that the only way you can live (because you can't live with this nauseous feeling) is up and down a spiral staircase in a slender lighthouse on an island out at sea.

—

Luckily, that was a misconception.

Grandma Is Sleeping

She got both glaucoma and cataracts early on in life, but she always managed, continued to crochet runners with tiny patterns, weave tapestries of small birds in a tangle of branches, colorful tulips twisting out of the soil and around each other, to the delight of her seven children and her seven children's spouses and her seven children's nineteen children. But today it bothers her. Today she stands at the kitchen window and looks up at the mountains and wishes she could distinguish where the mountains finish and the sky begins. She had such a strange dream last night, it's still vibrating somewhere inside, she's trying to understand her dream; she dreamed that the sun moved, or rather, slid, slowly, along the ridge of the mountains, while she sat in the kitchen and watched the sun slide, ever so slowly, at such an odd pace, first over one mountain, then the other, and then finally the third before disappearing out of sight. It was as though the sun was skating along the mountains, as though it had contact with the substratum, as though it had stepped down from the sky, as though it was peeping in at her, sailing along the mountain ridge, all the way along, to look in at *her* through the kitchen window, that the sun wanted to see. That it slipped over the mountains to look at her. That she herself was standing at the kitchen window looking at the sun. And that they were somehow measuring each other up. Then the sun disappeared. She was still shaking, because she felt it was a prophetic dream, it was the kind of dream she had had twice before, once when she was a young girl and dreamed about a bird that was hypnotized by a snake. That the bird was frozen in midair and just stared the snake in the eye, the snake that had uncoiled up from the ground and stood steady as a rod and held the bird's gaze. Soon after, she had met the boy she married. The second dream was much later, after she had given birth to seven children who had grown up and settled on farms round about, all seven of them, and produced nineteen children; she dreamed that she was sitting by the kitchen window and saw her husband descend from heaven in a long white robe with his hands folded on his chest. He floated slowly down as he looked her steadily in the eye, until he was standing on the ground in front of her. Soon after that, he died. And their seven children and nineteen grandchildren did all they could to keep her company, they popped by at regular intervals, sat at the kitchen table and did crosswords, chatted, and it was nice, but she sometimes got the feeling that they came more for their own sake than hers, that they were salving their conscience. That they were so busy, that they had such full lives and she just sat there, day in and day out, at the kitchen table and crocheted, wove. Looked out the window. But it didn't matter. They came, after all. And she sat there.

~

She looks out the window, can't differentiate the mountains from the sky. She's ninety today, and sees the first guests coming over the fields. She has set the table for everyone, used all the tables in her little house, put them all together. Found all the chairs and stools. She tries to count the shadows that are approaching, but can't, she recognizes her sons and their wives by their walks, and some of the grandchildren. One is carrying a baby. Or is it a cake tin? She pulls the finely crocheted lace curtains. Hears them tramping up the steps, grasping the door handle. Trying the door. Knocking. She doesn't move. The doorbell rings. She sees more people approaching, they're often on time, her flock, she'll give them that. There's a knock on the door. A rattling of the door handle. But she sits still. She doesn't want to open it. She's not ready, she thinks it's the dream that's taken hold of her, she's not finished with it, she wants to be alone. She sees their shadows darken the window, they knock, call her name. All of her family. But she won't open up.

An Entire Family Disappears

THE GRANDUNCLE (*stands up in the middle of the wake. Taps his glass with a spoon*)

AN ENTIRE FAMILY (*holds its breath*)

AN ENTIRE FAMILY (*fumbles with the napkins, knows what this particular granduncle is capable of. The candles flicker, tiny gusts of wind from the half-open windows ruffle the hair on the nervous heads of* AN ENTIRE FAMILY)

THE GRANDUNCLE (*clears his throat*)

THE GRANDUNCLE (*says something that makes* AN ENTIRE FAMILY *suddenly realize that their newly buried mother, grandmother, and great-grandmother had been sexually active*)

AN ENTIRE FAMILY (*drops its eyes to the floor*)

THE GRANDUNCLE (*persists. Tells something that makes* AN ENTIRE FAMILY *suddenly realize that it was a close shave that their newly buried mother, grandmother, and great-grandmother married their late father, grandfather, and great-grandfather*)

AN ENTIRE FAMILY *(drinks blueberry juice, the last blueberry juice found in her cupboard, and reflects on this, perhaps remembers something about a summer in the 1920s when they were engaged, a summer when she was not with him, when she was haymaking on the island Innlandet, and that she always had a particularly happy expression on her face when she talked about that summer)*

THE GRANDUNCLE *(articulates their thoughts. Tells them that after the summer haymaking on Innlandet, she sent the gold ring and watch that* AN ENTIRE FAMILY's *father, grandfather, and great-grandfather had given to her as an engagement present back to* AN ENTIRE FAMILY's *father, grandfather, and great-grandfather)*

THE GRANDUNCLE *(holds out his hand, imitates the movements of* AN ENTIRE FAMILY's *father, grandfather, and great-grandfather, as he stood with desperation in his eyes in front of his own father,* AN ENTIRE FAMILY's *grandfather, great-grandfather, and great-great-grandfather)*

AN ENTIRE FAMILY *(pictures the gold ring and watch cradled in the outstretched hand of their father, grandfather, and great-grandfather, flashing in the sunlight under the somber eyes of their grandfather, great-grandfather, and great-great-grandfather, sometime in the 1920s)*

AN ENTIRE FAMILY *(suddenly understands the*

truth about their own lives: they could just as easily have not been here)

THE GRANDUNCLE: But everything turned out for the best, as we know.

THE GRANDUNCLE: Hehehe.

AN ENTIRE FAMILY *(laughs politely)*

AN ENTIRE FAMILY *(hopes that the granduncle will stop talking soon, or at least say something less controversial. They are angry and upset)*

It's Raining in Love

Roar is terminally ill.

But he doesn't want to talk about it.

"No," Roar says. "I don't want to talk about it."

He looks out the living room window. A snail with a yellow shell drags itself slowly over the glass on the outside, leaving behind a shiny trail across the copper beech, which is in its prime, leaves shimmering in the evening light. It's summer. "Period," he says, then leans forward and taps the lowest drop on Grandma's crystal chandelier. It tinkles gently. "Do you know what happened to Henrik the other day?" he asks. "No," I say. "He was out walking . . ." Roar looks at me, asks me not to look at him like that, he's said he doesn't want to talk about it, and that's that, he's going to tell me about Henrik now, and what happened to Henrik the other day. "Are you happier with how I'm looking at you now?" I ask. He nods. "Henrik was out walking," he starts. And then tells me about what happened to Henrik when he was out walking—that he yawned just under a low branch and ended up with a tangle of tiny spiders in his mouth— while I look at his eyes, which are big and light, light blue, with long lashes, and think that he seems to be gazing inward, it's as if he can hardly bear to look at me, even though he is looking at me, that his irises are actually at the back, that they're in fact looking inward, into his head, and I wonder why he doesn't want to talk about it, even though there's perhaps not that much to say. Maybe he thinks it would be too much for me, that one of us might start to cry, and that the other wouldn't know how to deal with it. Even though we grew up together and know each other inside out, and have flicked the lowest drop on Grandma's old crystal chandelier to hear it tinkling a thousand times before. He's just hung it up. I gave it to him when I arrived, I wanted him to have it, thought that if he could tap the lowest drop and hear it tinkle . . . When he looks out the window that way his eyes are almost transparent, and his face is so pale, so pale that he's almost black. "Ugh," I say. "You've got that look again," he says. "How about now?" I say, and raise my eyebrows as high as I can, while squinting. Roar smiles, we almost laugh. "Did you hear about Ole's friend?" I ask, and he says that he hasn't. "It's not nice, just warning you," I say. "Well, come on then," he says. "He was out on his motorbike, had just come out of a tunnel when a bird flew straight into his chest, and then, because of the air drag, the bird was pushed up into his helmet, under the base gasket and into the helmet, dead and bloody, and Ole's friend threw up instantly, inside the helmet, everything happened so fast, he wobbled along the road for a few meters before he managed to stop the bike, then pulled off his helmet, which was full of bird and vomit, ran down to the fjord and ducked his head in the salt water," I say, and feel my heart racing because I said that the bird had died, I have to look at the floor. "Yuck," Roar said. "I found a huge white maggot in a Toblerone once," he says. "In the letter *R*." "No more Toblerone," I say, and bite my lip. Everything I say seems to come out wrong. But Roar laughs and says: "No, it's a shame. It's given me a complex about the first letter of my name, as well. Which is even more of a shame. I took it symbolically and thought that it must be a sign, simple as that; that my name is home to a huge white maggot. I'm thinking about changing my name." "To what?" I ask. "Joar," he says. "Well, you'd better change the last *R* too," I say. "*Joaj*." We laugh. "Just think, your name means loud noise in English," I say. "Yes, just *think*," Roar says, and I think about it and realize that I've said the wrong thing again, as his name will soon mean silence, was that what he meant?

"Do you want some whiskey?" he asks, and I say that I think it tastes of soap. Roar snorts, pours some whiskey. "Cheers," Roar says. "Cheers," I say, and take a sip. I shake my head without thinking. Roar smiles. "But I like the burning sensation in your throat," I say. We sit in silence and drink whiskey. "To continue with our cavalcade of disastrous events," Roar says, after a while, "I watched a magpie land in her nest in the apple tree down there, and then a raven came along and killed her." "I didn't know that ravens killed other birds," I say. "No, but then you're a person who thinks whiskey tastes like soap," Roar says, and I have to look out the window to hide how thrilled I am that he said just that. It would be embarrassing if he knew how happy comments like that made me in a very special and hopeful way. It would be embarrassing if he knew that I was in love with him. "The raven pecked out all her feathers, dismembered her, and then only took the bits he wanted." "That's a bit cynical," I say. "That's nature," Roar says. "And nature is cynical." "Uncle Arve found a swallow once," I say, "that was lying stone dead on its eggs. She'd killed herself brooding." "Once," Roar said, interrupting me, pouring himself more whiskey, eyes open wide, "once our kittens were eaten by a tomcat that had managed to sneak into the cellar." "Yes, because otherwise it was Uncle Arve who bashed them on the head." And we have to laugh. I look at his hand holding the glass, think that

I want it in my hair; his hands are thinner, they're about to fade into thin air, there's probably something perverse about me being turned on by them, even now, despite everything, I should be ashamed, they pull a cigarette from the pack in his breast pocket, they put the cigarette between his lips, I want them to leave the cigarette hanging from his lips, want them to bury themselves in my hair, from the neck up. But it's too late to think that now. We don't touch each other like that. We hug each other, we kiss each other on the cheek, we nudge each other in the ribs, we pat each other on the back. But we don't bury our hands in each other's hair, from the neck up. We don't stand looking into each other's eyes without saying anything anymore. Especially not now. That might make us cry. And in any case, we always say something. "Listen," I say suddenly, "there's something I have to tell you." I stop, feel my mouth getting drier and drier. But I have to do it now. "You know in films, how they often sit like we are and dread, dread what they have to say, so they say something else, that they haven't hung up the washing, or something like that, or they tell each other what they're dreading saying with a story about a friend." Roar gives me a dark look. "Do you think that's what I've been doing now, this evening? I said I don't want to talk about it." "I know, it's not that, it's something else." "Okay," Roar says. He waits. I look at him, take a deep breath, and say: "Well, all right. It *was* that." Roar shakes his head. "To think that your name means 'I've forgotten to hang up the washing' in English." "Yeah, imagine," I say and laugh a little, saved.

—

"The lightbulb in my bathroom has blown," he says after a while, and lights a cigarette. "At night it's dark there in a really weird way, I can stand for ages looking at everything in there, the towels hanging from the hooks, the toothbrush in the glass, the toothpaste, the razor, the shower curtain, and it's like I'm not in the room, like I shouldn't be there, like I'm seeing things how they are when I'm not there, do you understand what I mean? And that I shouldn't be, that somehow I'm a hindrance, but that's almost *why* I stay there." I nod, feel frightened, he's talking about it now, and I want him to stop. "And I like it," he says. He looks at me. "Are you feeling horny, or what?" he asks, tilting his head. "What?" I say. "You're stroking yourself on the thigh. You always do that when you've had a drink," he says, and I have to look out the window again. "It's just nature," I mumble, "and nature is cynical." He laughs. "Do you remember the time I hit you with some plastic tubing I found behind the house?" he asks, and I say what I always say, that I can't remember, that I must have suppressed it, that it must have been so awful that I've decided to obliterate it, and what kind of kinky association is this anyway— "And I got ill," Roar says, "after, it was the guilt, I had to stay in bed for two days and eat glucose tablets. And you came to visit me, but couldn't sit on the edge of the bed." We laugh. It starts to rain. Roar opens the window. "Come and hear," he says. I go over to him, look out at the garden and the apple tree, the white bench, and listen to the rain falling on the copper beech. Murmuring. Tingling. My neck is tingling. He puts his arms around me, pulls me in, my cheek against his chest. This is more than I can bear. This is the drop that makes me run over. I ask if he can run his hand through my hair, from the neck up. "Hmm?" he says. I ask if he can run his hand through my hair, from the neck up. "Hell, no," he says. "But as it's you . . ." And then he does it, he puts his hand in my hair and pulls it through from the neck up. Leans his forehead against mine. This is the closest he's been. He has his hand in my hair. But all I can feel is my throat burning, burning. "He's got the whole world," he sings. "Idiot," I say in a hoarse voice, but then laugh a little, so he knows I don't mean it.

Compulsion

The audience has settled in the auditorium. A voice over the loudspeaker asks everyone to turn off their mobile phones. The darkness descends slowly over their heads and shoulders. Sinks over arms that touch here and there, spreads down over the red plush seats and bags that have been placed between feet, over shoelaces, then someone coughs, someone clears their throat as though they may never get another chance. They are here to listen to a one-hour monologue, Andreas is about to take the stage. He is sitting on the steps behind the thick curtains, he looks onto the stage, which is completely bare except for a pair of shoes that are glued to the floor. The shoes and a small area around them will be illuminated by a pool of light in a few seconds. Andreas will slip his bare feet into the shoes and stand for an hour without moving, and talk. A great physical challenge awaits him; after a while he will start to feel dizzy and possibly lose all feeling in his legs. But he'll cope; he's spoken to the

Royal Guards at the palace and learned a few smart tricks for how to deal with it.

—

The curtains open, a spotlight focuses on the shoes in the middle of the stage. Andreas is still sitting hidden on the stairs, or, to be more precise, he is sitting curled around his own body, he's holding his knees, someone comes over and whispers, *Now*, but Andreas shows no sign of having heard what was said to him. He holds on to his own body on the stairs.* The

---

Floating

At the same time, far away, in Andreas's hometown, the doorbell rings at Andreas's father's house. From his position in the living room, he can see that it's someone selling raffle tickets, a little boy in a pom-pom hat who has no doubt been sent out by the local Bible group or sports club, or sent out by his mother to sell the tickets that *she* was supposed to sell for the local Bible group or sports club. It's snowing very lightly, and the raffle ticket seller rings the bell again. But because at some point in the 1970s, Andreas's father's right side started to curl in on itself, like leaves sometimes curl up when they wither—in on themselves toward the center—that is to say, his right leg and arm started to pull toward each other from the back, which in turn meant that the left side had to help, so that his arms and legs could meet, and as a result he now constantly has to lie on his stomach, as through the 1980s his hands and legs became more and more tightly entwined, and he folded in on himself like a flower that closes its petals at night and then over the years has ossified into this position; like a night-closed flower, he can't get up and open the door. The man is just one great knot. It's not so strange that he sometimes thinks life is a bit hard to bear, or worries what kind of attitude his situation may have instilled in his children, or that he sometimes looks forward to the day when someone will spread him as ash to the wind. Floating!

person gives up, shrugs to someone else who is standing farther away clasping his brow, to show that it's
impossible. The person holding his brow takes a couple
of resolute steps toward Andreas, who is sitting curled
around his own body, and silently shakes Andreas's
arms, trying to open a gap between Andreas's upper
body and thighs, but doesn't succeed. He makes an
obscene gesture in front of Andreas's eyes, which are
probably looking down at a step. Then he does a kind
of pirouette around himself, silently throws up his
hands, goes over to the other person, who has watched
this performance with a rather disinterested look on
his face. They walk away.

—

In the meantime, people have started to titter about
the pair of shoes in the middle of the stage that have
not been filled by anyone. The fact that it's taken so
long, and is still taking time, that nothing has happened yet, seems to amuse them, they probably see it
as an allusion to other plays, largely from the postwar
period. And after the first wave of laughter comes the
first silence, Andreas knows the pattern; the uncer-
tainty spreads; something is not right after all, maybe
it's not supposed to be like this, maybe we laughed
too soon. They rummage for sweets, they check that
they HAVE turned off their mobile phones, which

they have of course done. Ragnhild has even taken out the battery! Then, after about ten minutes, the first person gets up and leaves, which then makes the most intellectual member of the audience burst into a loud solo laughter that echoes around the auditorium, to show everyone that he has understood. (And this is what he has understood, or rather, these are the associations that now make him laugh: He sees the performance as a commentary on the futility of existence. There is a pair of empty shoes on the stage, they don't move, no one moves, the stage has been empty for ten minutes now, which has provoked the audience to start moving, in other words THE AUDIENCE IS NOW GETTING TO ITS FEET, and in a while the auditorium will be as empty as the shoes, but precisely BECAUSE the stage has not been able to produce a movement, a being; a pair of legs, a person. In other words, in some strange and paradoxical way, art has interfered with life and done something to it. In other words, art has conveyed a moral, and my goodness, it's been a long time since there was evidence of the will to do that, and if he, a member of the audience, were to call this form of theater anything, he would absolutely and without a doubt call it action theater. He's enjoying the obvious paradox!) And the others think about it and decide that it's actually quite funny, and deeply tragic. In the meantime, another person has gone over to Andreas and asked him in as quiet a hiss as possible if Andreas could PLEASE get a GRIP on himself, that this can't carry on much longer, that he'll get the boot if he doesn't pull himself together. Andreas sits curled around his body and doesn't move, thinks if they just wait *for fifteen minutes*. But there is no way for Andreas to communicate this to the person, because if he does, terrible things will happen, the world as we know it will collapse. He can't say a word until fifteen minutes are up. The person walks away. Makes a movement with his hands, and the curtains close. Before fifteen minutes have passed. As usual. A thunderous applause erupts. Finally, Andreas stands up and goes out onto the stage to receive his applause, as if it's something he has to do. He shrugs apologetically, opens the curtains just enough, puts his big toe into the shoe as if he were dipping it in water, quickly pulls his foot back as though the water were cold, laughs a little, then gives another apologetic shrug, the audience applauds, Andreas bows, exits left in twelve long strides and steps on the last gap between the planks perfectly, he has to hit it in such a way that the gap divides the sole of his foot in two.

Oh, Life

Innovation

Eve is the name of a woman who has opened her legs for a man. His name is Frank. Frank has a nice cock, Eve thinks. His cock goes in and out of her and she thinks it's very nice.

—

Three days ago, Frank's cock was going in and out of a woman called Gerd; Gerd had big, round breasts that Frank cupped while he stood behind her, moving his cock in and out.

—

Three days before that, Gerd was kneeling on her bed letting another man's cock go in and out of her; his name was Adam. Adam held her hips rather than her breasts and said, Oh God, Oh God. All aquiver he asked Gerd if she could reach her hand back, if she could get hold of his balls, if she could stroke them. Twelve hours earlier, he had been standing behind a woman who was called Eve, saying, Oh God, Oh God, while Eve supported herself with one hand and stroked his balls that were slapping against her buttocks with the other.

—

Now Eve is doing the same for Frank, and with great success. Oh God, he says.

—

God listens, he thinks. Then he makes everything apart from this disappear. The weather, time, the economy, those pointless conversations in the line at the deli, rose-growing, umbrella-buying, waiting in banks, all professions, all train departures and bus routes, bumping into someone unexpected around the corner, watching someone eat breakfast and suddenly being overwhelmed by love, by the feeling that one wants to remain here forever, in this ridiculously dec- orated room with large windows where someone is eating their breakfast, and one only has to reach out a hand to stroke the other person's hair and not say a thing, in short, to love someone, etc.—all the usual pillars that in their own unremarkable and impressive ways have held everything together. They vanish. The practical consequences are that the world is now different, more horizontal, men and women have to have sex with each other all the time.* It's a bit like a relay, or musical chairs, but everyone gets one and no one is left out. In a way, society has never been more intertwined even though all the usual pillars have fallen.

---

*Manual
If you want to change partners and you are a man, simply pull out your cock, push the man who is moving his cock in and out of the woman/man you have chosen aside, and then take his place. The woman/man who has been pushed aside has to roll over and push aside the woman/man who is kneeling in front of another man and take his/her place. If he or she meets with resistance, he or she must bite and pinch. This always has positive results.

Echo

Arild Eivind Bryn was a demon at selling encyclopedias.

—

Arild Eivind Bryn was success in its purest and rawest
form. Put it this way, Bjarte Bø said, the man's hand-
shake leaves its mark. He was young, free, had it all.
A job with a salary that fed itself fat on the way to
heaven, a nippy little Italian model with four idolized
wheels, and a huge flat in one of the best parts of
town. He had a legendary serve that had helped him
smash his way to the top of the company's tennis
tournament, in summer he went climbing in Switzer-
land with the boys' club, Conquistadors of the Mound
of Venus, and if someone had decided to tap Arild
Eivind Bryn's heart, it would have pumped out the
finest chateau wine. The only thing that might detract
from the Bryn phenomenon was his first name, a

somewhat unusual combination that was the result
of a fierce patriarchal fight. But even the name Arild
Eivind was a success, it was a personal gimmick. His
friends liked to hear themselves say it. It was as if they
were part of something then. Part of it. *There.*

—

And what's more, Arild Eivind was nice, *damn* nice,
Bjarte Bø said. Bjarte Bø looked up to Arild Eivind
Bryn. *Damn*, he thought, when he thought of Arild
Eivind. Tone didn't like him swearing so much, you
never did before, she often said, and Bjarte would reply: I don't swear that often, damn it, and so got Tone
to laugh it all off.

—

Tone was the one area where he felt he had the better
of Arild Eivind. It was an area that Arild Eivind had
not yet explored. Not even surveyed. Where he had not
yet become chairman of the board, no distinctions
here, no trophies. Bjarte, on the other hand, would
soon have the papers ready, and gold around his finger to prove it. That is, until the moment when Arild
Eivind had looked over his shoulder at him, on his way
to a lunch meeting, file tucked under his arm, swinging

out through the office door, his hair flopping slightly to the right as he turned toward Bjarte:

"Better to have a girl on every floor than to be stuck with one in the elevator."

After that, Bjarte always took the stairs.

—

"*Damn*," Bjarte muttered, savoring the sight of Arild Eivind's nippy little Italian parked by the curb.

"*The man muttered under his breath*," Tone said, half irritated, half to the wind, which partly swallowed her voice that took off, took flight toward the end of the sentence. "Hmm?" said Bjarte.

"Just a quote," said Tone. "Joyce," she added, but she knew it was needless, pointless, hopeless. A sense of duty, perhaps, on her part, maybe, to tell him something he didn't know, and that he didn't care he didn't know.

"You and your quotes," Bjarte said, and for a moment was proud, she could impress with her quotes, he thought, at the table. He looked at the car again. When his wallet was fat enough, he was going to get a car like that, just like that: a lively, little lean machine. He couldn't think of anything he wanted more.

"Bad parking," Tone said and pointed at the front wheel that was on the curb. "Looks like a dead-drunk man propping himself up with his elbow." She laughed. Bjarte decided not to be offended. Nothing was going to ruin his state of elation. Today his friendship with Arild Eivind would climb another level. They had been invited for a Sunday meal. Arild Eivind was going to make it himself, he was a master at Italian, he said. And he wanted to meet Tone. Bjarte was ecstatic. "Wear the black dress, you look great in that," he said, as Tone stood in front of the mirror, studying her face, with two lipsticks in her hand. He put on the blue shirt he'd just bought, which he was particularly pleased with. Curled his toes against the floor.

—

Tone walked beside him, she looked great and annoyed. She had a headache, there was northerly wind blowing, it licked her neck with its icy, greedy tongue. She didn't like that kind of wind. She didn't like that kind of car. That kind of parking. It symbolized something she couldn't stand. Attitude. A way of being. She saw Bjarte's face tense in anticipation as they got closer to the door, it was five o'clock, and the wind was blowing up the split, the long split in her dress, up and around her knees. "*Damn*," Bjarte said and rang the bell.

—

No response.

—

"We're not too early, are we?" Bjarte said, and Tone could see on her watch that they weren't. They were on time. "Must be something keeping him at the stove," he said, and liked what he'd said, Tone would think this man was a conscientious cook, a man who didn't just leave his pots at the most important point in the process, a good quality, he thought, and put his arm around her, he was friends with a man of good qualities, it had to rub off, make him even better in her eyes, Bjarte would never leave his pots at the most important point in the process either, just to open the door. He stroked his thumb over her shoulders.

—

Still no reaction.

—

"*Damn*," Bjarte muttered, starting to feel uneasy, and he forced himself to ring the bell several times in succession, which he immediately regretted, so finished off with a long, reasonable, and manly ring. Suddenly the door opened, and a pair of eyes squinted out from under a mop of blond hair. Arild Eivind was in his underpants and scratched his chest, he couldn't see anything, he said, his eyes were full of sand: he rubbed them, opened them, saw them, and said, "*Fuck.*"

"Is it Sunday today?" he asked, then noticed Tone, and nodded and smiled: "Hi!"

"Yes," Bjarte said, as Tone mumbled hi.

"Late night last night," Arild Eivind said, and shook his head, and Bjarte said, "*Ah*," in an understanding way. "*Ah*," Bjarte said again, and Arild Eivind nodded, then slapped his forehead as he turned.

"Sorry, welcome, dear guests, come in," Arild Eivind said.

When their host was dressed, Tone saw where Bjarte had gotten the idea of blue shirts. And following a trip to the bathroom: the clean-shaven jaw. "Oh, that won't do," Arild Eivind said when he realized that both he and Bjarte were standing there in blue shirts, with fair hair cut in more or less the same style—Bjarte had more gel in his. Then he laughed and clapped Bjarte on the arm. "I'll go and put a white one on." Bjarte curled his toes against the floor.

—

They sat in the living room for a while, and Arild Eivind apologized and Bjarte said that it was fine, and a new plan was hatched: Arild Eivind would take

at the Edge of the Forest

tood at the edge of the forest and was mis-
felt like there was no point in anything,
ght as well give up. I walk around here, day
y out, the deer thought, and there's no one
me. Am I invisible, or what? He didn't think
around here and could change people's lives
ould only see me, but no one sees me. Here
hart, and no one cares. The *whole point* is
m supposed to be difficult to see, I know that,
pposed to roam around in the forest and not
. But it's the very premise of my life that is now
me miserable. I want to be seen. So here I am
edge of the forest. I am open to being seen, to
shot. If someone doesn't see me soon, I'm going
something drastic, I mean it. Right now it feels
m trapped in deerness. Oh, I would love to
e everything, be someone else, something com-
y different. Oh, imagine if I could be a roe deer,
k.

them out to a restaurant. He had given them a glass of mineral water, shared a painkiller with Tone, and let them listen to a new recording of Satie's three *Gymnopédies* that he'd just bought, and that he was particularly pleased with. Tone remembered one of the pieces from a series that had been shown on children's TV in the summer, it made her sad. "Yes," Arild Eivind said, "so deliciously melancholy."

—

"I'll call for a taxi," Arild Eivind said, "the car's parked about half an hour away."

Bjarte was taken aback. "But your car's parked right outside."

"*Huh?*" Arild Eivind exclaimed. "Are you *sure?*" He went over to the window, looked down, and started to laugh. "Did I drive it? I can't remember that at all, *at all, fucking hell*," he laughed, and Bjarte laughed with him. "*Jesus, Arild Eivind*," he laughed, and slapped him on the back. "*Jeeez-sus*," and Tone thought to herself in exasperation that Bjarte was taking in Arild Eivind like a leaking boat and she wasn't sure she wanted to carry on bailing.

—

"Yes, really good," Bjarte repeated.

The lighting in the restaurant was dim, the small tea lights in the tea light holders made of glass cast a warm flickering glow over the small-check tablecloths whenever someone spoke or laughed. They had talked a little more about Satie, and then Tone had said something about "poetry," and Arild Eivind had pointed at the tea lights in the glass holders and said: "I remember reading somewhere that someone said poetry was like the glow of a flame under glass."

Tone looked at him, suitably impressed. "And when glass itself is in a flame?" she asked.

"That would be creation itself, then, wouldn't it?" Arild Eivind said.

They looked straight at each other. Said nothing. The waiter appeared with more mineral water, and Bjarte, with too much wine in his blood, who had dropped out of the conversation a while back, sat with a fixed smile that hovered above the tablecloth. Fumbling and mumbling, he wanted to talk about encyclopedias and sex. "*Fuck's sake, Tone.*" He said it too loud and she asked him to be quiet.

"Why do *you* have so much to talk about, I don't remember you even knowing each other," he muttered. "Resonance," Arild Eivind replied, and once his left hand had put down the licked-clean fork on his plate where the steel prongs could cool, it slipped under the table and stole up the long split in her dress and

she was more cons
for a long time. She
a brittle, reassuring
like hers, and it daw
ber, she couldn't ev
looked like.

The Deer

The deer
erable. H
like he m
in and d
who sees
so. I wal
if they c
I am, a
that I ar
I am su
be seen
making
at the
being
to do
like I
chang
plete
an el

It's Snowing

In the narrow cobbled streets, in the dark, in the light from the streetlamps, it looks as though the snow is standing still. The puddles on the asphalt sparkle. And around the corner, into Øvregata, comes Thomas with a tightly rolled newspaper in his hand. He says something about the snow. That it's almost standing still. And that *The Mirror* by Andrei Tarkovsky is his favorite film. He remembers that the wind was blowing in the opening scene, that there was a lot of wind (he gesticulates with his arms and the hand holding the newspaper, imitating the wind blowing through tall cornfields), and that they were sitting on a fence that then collapsed. And the disappointment when the girl realizes that the person who came through the tall grass, or corn, was not the one she was sitting on the fence waiting for, but someone else. Thomas looks down. I ask if we should maybe find a café. There's something about this snow, Thomas says. It's snowing so damn quietly. It reminds me of something.

—

We sit in a café that is just below street level, the sidewalk starts at about our waist, we sit there like halved mannequins in a big window facing out onto a street that runs down a long slope, Thomas says the snow reminds him of Helene. He folds the newspaper, wedges it under one of the table legs, so the table is steady, and I think about Helene, it hurts when I do, I see the soft, strange light around her, her eyes that are so big, so black with eyeliner, that look as if they're about to cry the whole time, even though she's happy or gazing blankly out the window, her fair hair that always looks as if it's about to blow away, I think about the whole of Helene, who I can now see standing in front of me like soft snow hanging in the air. Thomas lifts the cup of coffee to his mouth and says that's the thing, that people come walking through windy fields, and they're not the ones you're sitting waiting for after all. And the times when you yourself come walking through windy fields (to stick with the same image, Thomas says), it's not often, in fact he can't remember it ever happening (with the exception of Helene, he says, looking down at the table), that you are the one that someone's sitting on the fence waiting for. That's the worst thing about windy fields. A third interpretation, Thomas says, and takes a sip of coffee, squeezing his eyes shut to ease the hotness, a third interpretation, he repeats, is that the one who comes walking is not even a person, but a memory, for example, an age. Oneself is a windy field. One has a fence that someone is sitting on, that is about to break. Windy fields, I say, shaking my head, should be banned. There should be a sign saying: "Wind—No Access." Or just: "FORGET IT." Thomas smiles. He recites a poem.

> *The gates are open*
> *The gates blow in the wind*
> *What's in there*
> *What are you offering me?*
> *Oh, always something!*
> *There's a little dust, some specks of dirt*
> *A broken cog on the earthen floor*
> *And some old slag left from an abandoned smithy*
> *That maybe was never there*

That maybe was never there, I repeat, squinting over my cup of coffee, I look at Anna, she has that shiny look in her eyes that she always gets when she listens to me recite poetry, I like her for that shininess, it makes her like Helene, that's maybe why I always associate the two of them, because otherwise they're not alike at all, but they have that shininess, a kind of transparency. I feel a pricking somewhere, I think about Helene, I think about the strange, soft light around her, her big black made-up eyes that always look as if they're about to cry even though they're not, even though she's laughing, even though she's just gazing blankly out the window, and I think of her tousled, feather-like hair that always looks like it's about to blow away. Anna sits with her hands around her teacup, her knuckles are red, her hands are not particularly beautiful, they look like they were made to pull up potatoes, to be dried on an apron, to be numb when it's cold, they're red and white, and even though there's something potato-like about them, there is something beautiful after all, I think and change my mind, they look fragile, there's something shiny about them, I look up at her hair, it's dark and curly, there are drops of water in it, it's shiny, her cheeks are red, she looks out the window. I remember another scene from a Tarkovsky film, Anna says, and looks at me again, a scene where the first thing you see, I don't remember it that well, but I think the first thing you see is the head of a man from behind, he's standing on a beach and looking out to sea, and then we see his face in profile as he bends down, then we follow his gaze, we see what he sees, we see his big face, his forehead, nose, mouth, chin, we see everything from his perspective; the sky, the sea, and then we look down onto the beach, the sand, a miniature house stands there, and the camera lets go of the man and we go right down onto the sand, and the camera stops, and all we see is the miniature house and the sand and the sea in the background, and if it hadn't been for the fact that we followed the man's gaze to begin with, we might well have thought that it was a full-sized house, Anna says, I've heard everything she said, but I was listening to her voice most of all, I feel a prickling on my neck, want to kiss her, think about kissing her, all of a sudden, have tried to keep that sort of thing at bay, I look at the snow, picture Helene, the strange, soft light, the pricking, prickling on my neck, I take another drink of coffee, too fast, it burns.

—

Is that Helene? I ask, and Thomas chokes on his coffee. Where? he asks, and I nod toward a woman walking along the sidewalk in the confoundedly silent snow. Hmm, Thomas says, and looks around. He glances over at her again. Looks like it, he says. Jeez. Helene is walking slowly. She's looking at the ground. She's wearing a plum red coat with a belt knotted around her waist that makes her look even thinner, and her fair, tousled hair that always looks like it's about to blow away looks like it's about to blow away. Thomas's cheeks and forehead are flushed, slightly panicked. Helene walks toward us, we can't hide, she'll see us, it's a long time since we saw her last, almost two years, we didn't know where she went, she just left, took her things with her, moved, and so it's a long time since she has seen us, the last time she saw us, she saw us in an awkward naked nearness on a sofa at half past five in the morning, on Helene's red sofa, in an unusual position for us; Thomas and I have spent a lot of time since then finding our way back to a kind of friendship, Thomas has lived without a sofa for a long time. Now she's walking toward us again, and we can't get away, we're prisoners at our table, Thomas bends down, pulls out the newspaper that is wedged under the table leg, while I sit paralyzed and stare at Helene, who hasn't seen us yet, how can she not see us? I wonder as Thomas opens the newspaper to hide his face and follows the long columns in detail while the fingers holding the paper tremble, I don't know what to do, I've got a teacup in my hands, I look down at my hands, which are red and white, red over the knuckles, they're not beautiful, I think, I don't dare look up, don't want to look up until Helene has passed, *maybe* she won't see us, the window where we're sitting is on a side street to the sidewalk Helene is walking along, *maybe* nothing will happen. I look at the teacup, at my hands that are red and white, and register that two gray trouser legs are now standing by the window, I see a plum red coat, I look up, see a belt tied around a waist, see Helene standing there, with a strange and soft light around her, with big black made-up eyes that always look like they're about to cry even though they're not, she's standing there with her hands in her pockets, her face blank, looking in at us. Thomas, I say. Thomas lowers the newspaper. Helene's eyes turn to Thomas. Then she takes a gun out of her pocket, opens her mouth, puts the gun in her open mouth, tilts her head back, Thomas sits paralyzed on his chair, staring, Helene pulls the trigger, nothing happens, she takes the gun out of her mouth again, puts it back in her pocket, shrugs, smiles at us, turns and carries on walking down the sidewalk.

—

Neither of us gets up and goes after her. We just watch the plum red coat get smaller and smaller until it eventually disappears around a corner. What are you offering me? Thomas says after a long time. I pick up my scarf, wrap it around my throat, stand up. Take out my mittens. Thomas folds the newspaper, puts it in his pocket. Pays. Stays sitting. I run my hands through my hair, feel that it's wet. Walk toward the door. Turn around, wait. Thomas is still sitting and looking out the window. Looking at the snow that's snowing as though it was night.

Fortune Smiles on Mona Lisa

When Mona Lisa was little, she had a red currant bush. It was Mona's dad who decided one day, he was standing in the living room, and looked from Mona Lisa to the garden to Mona Lisa, who was, small and pale, sitting in a corner with a book on her lap, and he said loudly, as he pointed out the window: That is Mona Lisa's red currant bush. Mona Lisa looked up. What? she said. From that day on, she waited for the red currants to ripen. She could sit in the garden for hours waiting. But nothing happened. First the snow had to melt, then the bush had to produce small white flowers, and then the tiny green berries had to swell, which then had to grow and get big, and transparent. Will they never get ripe? she asked her father. And her father said yes. They will turn bright red and gleam in the sun, her father said. But will they still be transparent? she asked; she liked the white, transparent berries. To an extent, her father said. Mona Lisa was impatient. If they're not going to get any bigger, just

change color, and when they're red only be transparent to an extent, why can't we just pick them now?
But her father was firm. Why do you absolutely want
them to be transparent? Because it's nice, Mona Lisa
said. Whatever the case, they're too sour now, Mona,
he said. But as he turned to go back to the house,
Mona Lisa reached out quick as lightning and picked
a white red currant, popped it in her mouth, and
chewed. And behind her father's back, who was now
walking up to the house at a leisurely pace, Mona
Lisa made a face and opened her mouth and dribbled, more than spat, the berry out as quietly as
she could.

—

But finally, one warm July day, it had happened. The
family came home from their holiday in Sweden, and
all the berries were sparkling red and to an extent
transparent. Mona Lisa leaped out of the car in only
her shorts, stopped in the middle of the garden when
she saw the gleaming red bush, clutched her hands in
front of her chest, and said: Oh! Then she spun around,
ran into the house to get a bowl, and ran back. It was
with a mixture of celebration and trepidation that
she nipped off a red berry, put it in her mouth, and
chewed. It was fresh and acidic, Mona Lisa was overwhelmed, she lifted her hands to the heavens and

closed her eyes. Then she picked, in almost ecstatic concentration. The bush was a triumph.

—

Suddenly she felt something tickling her thigh. She looked down and saw a huge man sitting there. She was gripped by fear. She tried to brush him off. But the man would not budge. It looked quite ridiculous: a huge man sitting on little Mona Lisa's thigh. Mona Lisa screamed and ran around the garden, in an attempt to get the man to fall off. But it was as if he was nailed there. It felt like it would never end, that she would run around the garden with a man nailed to her thigh forever, she started to run toward the house: Daddy, Daddy!

—

Her father removed the man with a pair of pliers, squashed him flat and threw him out to the cats, then comforted the howling Mona Lisa. After that, she wanted nothing to do with the red currant bush, and left the others in the family to do the picking.

—

That was all a long time ago. Right now, Mona Lisa is crossing the road at a zebra crossing in a dark and cold town, the streetlights are lit and it's late October, or thereabouts. She is forty-one and she's trying to get a man out of her head, but she can't. In Mona Lisa's head there remains, as though nailed there: a mouth that is the softest mouth, not big, but good, dark hair that is the softest, darkest hair, a pair of hands, a back, a pair of eyes that are the lightest, bluest eyes ever. And more: the ears, neck, chin, throat, shoulders, arms, chest muscles, nipples, stomach, cock, thighs, kneecaps, lower legs, buttocks, and foot soles of this man, who is actually more of a boy, not particularly tall, one of her pupils, in fact. A young, wise person she has slept with habitually, but now she wants him out of her head, and not to sleep with him anymore. It has to stop. She loves him, he doesn't love her, I don't just want sex! thinks Mona Lisa, that's not what I'm like, she is not a modern, liberated woman, she just wants to be loved. She crosses the road and is miserable. The streetlights illuminate her face, and it's a sad face.

—

A man comes cycling by on the other side of the road. Mona Lisa follows him with her eyes, she's seen him before, he's been in some ads that she's seen at the cinema, for instant soup, and otherwise she's seen him roller-skating around town, wearing a string vest, high on something. But now he's on a low black bike, and she thinks he's beautiful, he's shaved off all his hair except for a ponytail that he's constructed into a tiny tower on the back of his head with the help of some string, and he's wearing the strangest clothes. And his eyes follow Mona Lisa as he cycles by. And at exactly the point where the two paths they've chosen through town intersect, a smile spreads over their faces, at the same time, it's as if their faces open, and they are astounded. Perhaps it wasn't much, but under the next streetlight, we see that the sadness in Mona Lisa's face has softened. In fact, we could even say that for a moment, perhaps, she was happy.

Deal

She's lying under a bush and cursing everything. Damned itchy hat, damned rain. Damned, fucking combination of wool and wet, damned bush, damned wet ground that makes her jeans *wet* that were already damp from before, damned down jacket that is wet and squeaks, damned darkness, damned fjord, damned sound of cars whooshing past down on the main road once every half hour or so, it's not exactly rush hour here after eleven. The last ferry has gone, she didn't make it, the ferry left the quay just as she came round the bend, she didn't have lights on her bike, they probably didn't see her, she'd cycled ten kilometers, ten fucking kilometers, in the bike's easiest gear, to get to the ferry, and she missed it. She'd grabbed her brother's old bike that had been standing in the garage since he left, she wasn't to know that the gears didn't work, she only found out after she'd been cycling for about a quarter of an hour and the whole system collapsed just as she was about to change into fourth, it was impossible to fix it, she knew nothing about bikes, she was just going to ride it, so she cycled in low third for ten fucking kilometers, she refused to give up now that she'd started; to escape, her legs spun furiously yet she was barely moving. On she crept, helmet and all, she got encouraging hoots from passing cars, she cursed them, lowered her head so they wouldn't see who it was. In the end she stopped, threw the helmet in a ditch, broke her nails when trying to pull the reflectors off the pedals, then carried on cycling, longing for a hill. She cycled ten kilometers like that, ten long kilometers along the fjord where nobody lived, and as she rounded the bend down to the quay, the ferry pulled out into the fog-darkened, drizzled fjord, into the night, without her, the quay was empty, the kiosk was closed, the shoreline along the ness silent and black, the lampposts each stood rooted in the tarmac that was empty, empty apart from her, and there was no fucking way she was going to cycle the ten kilometers back, no way, she had run away, escaped, SPLIT, she had left behind fish-cake hell when Aunt Alma had gone to bed for the night and rolled over onto her stomach so that her flannel nightie twisted around her body, she had thought I'm just going to do it, now, I've thought about it every night, and I'm just going to do it, I'll take the bike and I'll just cycle away from here. She was going to be so cool, never again would she smell fish cakes, and she would start swearing, she had all the swearwords saved up inside, but had never said them out loud. She was going to start now; but first she was going to catch the ferry out of here, then she was going to start swearing. A simple plan. Someone could fix the bike on the ferry. She would just carry on cycling on the other side, without knowing where she was going, she wasn't quite sure exactly where in Norway the ferry came in, on the other side, but she thought it eventually linked up with the road to Ålesund, but it didn't matter, what mattered was that she had escaped the damned house, the damned old sofa, the damned worn linoleum floor with scrunched-up rag rugs, run away from the stuffy, rancid smell of fish cakes, the cool feeling of the Respatex table against her arms every damn morning, she'd thought, as she stood and watched the last ferry in the world disappear out into the fjord, into the night, leaving her all alone at the edge of the universe, she thought, and almost started to cry. She looked over at the parking place, Alvin's old van was standing there, but Alvin wasn't inside, he must have gone up to Susanne's, who lived in the last house before the ferry, all on its own, up on the slope, the light was on, which made her think that Susanne also lived on the edge of the universe, Susanne who caused a drama at every church sale, according to her aunt, because people always divided into two camps, one that supported Alvin's wife and one that supported Susanne—and *that* was only Susanne herself, her aunt said and laughed, she sympathized with Susanne as she stood there, sympathized with the light in the house, she sympathized with the black, silent ness that stretched out into the fjord like a friendly finger pressed to the water's lips saying, Shhh, and she almost started crying, she most definitely was not going to cycle home, she refused, she would find a bush up on the slope and lie under it and sleep until morning, when she could take the first ferry across.

—

She lies under the bush and has no idea what time it is. She has a watch, but it's too dark for her to see it, she has the feeling it would be easier to wait if she knew HOW much longer she had to wait, now that she has to wait for a wet, dark eternity that smells of rotting leaves and earth. It smells of rain, her jacket gives off loud squeaks, she doesn't like the way things have gone, that she's scared of the noise, that generally she's just a little frightened, she realizes. She doesn't know what time it is, it bothers her, she would love to know what time it is, if she went down onto the road she could find out, she could just jump up onto the road, hold her arm up under a streetlight and see what time it is, it might even be possible to see before she gets to the road, the glow from the streetlights might be strong enough, she'll try anyway, she'll get up at least from the ground that's now seeping in through her trousers, she stands up. She's cold right through, stiff, her bike is lying in the ditch, she feels quite affectionate when she sees it, she touches the handlebars, scrambles up the bank to the road, over the crash barrier, pulls up her sleeve, looks at her watch: it's a quarter past twelve. A quarter past twelve! Not later! FUCK, she screams. Damn, she says. She looks around, the fjord frightens her. It's pitch-black. She hears rustling. The bush where she's been hiding frightens her. It's all black. She scrambles back down into the ditch, picks up the bike, struggles not to slip back down the embankment, but manages to get up, lifts the bike over the crash barrier. But she can't get started in bottom third. She pushes the bike homeward.

—

Suddenly she hears the sound of a car behind her, she wonders if she should jump down into the ditch, but it's too late, the car pulls up alongside her, it's Alvin's van, Alvin sticks his head out the window, his cheeks are red, he clears his throat. "So, here you are in the middle of the night," he says. "Well, so are you, by the looks of it," she says, and he doesn't reply. "Problem with the bike?" he asks, and she tells him the gears aren't working, something happened when she was going to shift up to fourth, the whole system collapsed and she couldn't fix it. "I'll drive you home," Alvin says, stops the van, puts the bike in the back, and she gets into the passenger seat. She's despondent, doesn't have anything to say, she's cycled ten kilometers in bottom third, missed the last ferry in the world, lain under a bush and gotten wet, and is now sitting in Alvin's van, who obviously has been at Susanne's, he's got a bite mark on his hand, it's red. "So, were you trying to keep fit?" Alvin asks, he doesn't look at her, and she doesn't look at him either, she looks out at the fjord, which lies there pitch-black, it's raining, she likes the sound of the windshield wipers. "No," she says. "Have you been at Susanne's?" she asks, it just pops out of her mouth, she didn't even have time to think. Alvin doesn't say anything for a while. She feels the heat from the seat warming her wet clothes, she leans her head back, still looking out at the fjord. "Why do you ask that?" he says. She nods at his hand. "You've got a bite mark on your hand." "Huh?" he says, and looks down. "Oh God," he says. He's quiet for a while. "Don't suppose you've got any makeup with you?" he asks, she has to laugh. "I'm afraid not," she says. She can see now that Alvin is desperate. His face is bright red and his forehead wrinkled right up to the hairline. He's gripping the steering wheel so hard that his knuckles are white, staring at the road ahead as if it might suddenly leap up and hit them. His jaw is clenched, his lips are trembling, and then Alvin starts to cry, quietly, his whole body sobs with tears, the van goes slower and slower, it's evident that Alvin can't see where he's going, because they're driving onto the other side of the road, "STOP," she shouts, as the front of the van veers over the midway marker, and Alvin jumps and slams on the brakes. The van stops.

—

The rain drums on the roof, Alvin puts his head down on the steering wheel, she just tries to listen to the windshield wipers, the quiet hum, the slight whine as they pull themselves over the window, she watches them, they make a pattern that's like Chinese fans. She doesn't know what to say, if she should try to comfort him. It feels absurd to be sitting in a van in the middle of the night with a forty-year-old man who is sobbing and crying, it's as if every fiber in her body is crippled by shyness, while Alvin slowly but surely stops crying and just sits there with his head on the wheel. "You coooouuuld . . . ," she starts, "you could say that it was me who did it, you could say you were driving along and you saw me cycling at full speed, out of control, swinging back and forth across the road . . . that I was shouting and crying and in a real state . . . that I was high on hash and ecstasy that I'd gotten from some guy . . . that you've noticed on the ferry, from the other side . . . a thin, creepy guy from

Ålesund . . . who I met on the quay and it looked like I bought something from him, and I was cycling around completely out of control, and you had to try to stop me and get me to come down before you drove me home because you didn't want me to get into trouble . . . and I was totally out of order, and you had to wrestle with me, I was wild, I shouted and swore and screamed, and then I bit you as hard as I could on the hand, you started to bleed, even, and now you have to take an AIDS test as soon as possible." She looks at him, he has a strange look on his face, as though he's struggling to hold back the laughter. "I *mean* it, Alvin," she says, and then Alvin starts to laugh, he laughs and laughs, and she can't understand why, she is hurt. "What?" she says. "Is it really that unlikely that I'd cycle around high on hash and ecstasy?" "No, no, no," Alvin says, but she can tell that it is, that it is utterly unlikely that she would cycle around, high on hash and ecstasy, and she thinks that maybe it's so funny, and wrong, because she said *two* drugs, so she says, "Well, or heroin then," and Alvin laughs even more, and now she's really hurt and upset about everything, and she starts to cry. Alvin stops laughing and takes her hand. "Don't cry," he says. "And you're telling me," she says. "Pah," Alvin says, and squeezes her hand, and says they have a deal. "*Deal*," Alvin says, and then he starts the van and they drive home along the fjord.

Trapeze

Frans Ekman creeps from his bed and looks out the window, where his own tiny piece of Bergen is revealed: a narrow street and a man walking his dog. The dog does his business as the man whistles at a woman in a purple suit who walks past. The man who whistles doesn't seem to be aware that the attention doesn't make the woman happy, only angry and upset. She suffers from a form of paranoia that means that she misinterprets everything: for example, if someone had said that her neat little purple suit was elegant and fitted her perfectly, she would think that they really thought it was horrible and that she had no taste, and was therefore pathetic. Because of her paranoid disposition, this woman once shot a man, her lover at the time, because she thought he was also fucking the caretaker's wife. She served her sentence. And now the petite woman thinks that she's had enough for today, yes, enough, she starts to cry, silently, but the man doesn't see, he has to pick up the dog shit, and he still thinks it's disgusting, even though he's done it so often that you would think he liked it perhaps just a little: a warm, moist consistency between the fingers, maybe even a little rub back and forth, inside the plastic bag.

—

The man then throws the bag of dog shit up onto Frans Ekman's small balcony with great confidence, as if his arm knows exactly how much force is needed for the bag to land on Frans Ekman's balcony. Frans Ekman stands in the window and exchanges a look with the man, who is Frans Ekman's brother. Then Frans Ekman opens the door to the balcony, without looking at his brother, picks up the bag, and, holding it between two fingers, walks straight through the flat, opens the door out into the hallway, goes out through the door, opens the cover in the wall opposite, and drops the bag of dog shit down the rubbish chute. Then he goes back into the bathroom. Washes his hands. Pulls off his pants, sits on the edge of the bath and suddenly feels that life is unbearable. That he can't carry on like this. That something has to change. Somewhere, somehow.

—

Frans Ekman looks down at his feet. The floor heating has made them glow; he gets into the bath, turns on the shower. The warm water soothes his body like a caress, and he stands completely still for a while, letting himself be caressed. Then he masturbates to an inner picture of the young girl downstairs who Lena is so jealous of because she's young, only seventeen, and also has large breasts, which of course Lena doesn't, and she's so blonde and beautiful and thin, unbelievably thin for having such large breasts, something's not right, Lena often says, it's not natural, she's cheated, and he simply has to understand that when he looks at her breasts, it's not breasts he's looking at, but two disgusting bags of silicone, and if that turns him on, well then maybe it's not breasts that turn him on, real breasts that is, at all; the real thing, and that is something totally different, has a life, has lived (like Lena, but Lena would never bring herself to say that, Lena is in no way young and thin, and perhaps not beautiful either). Lena is Frans Ekman's "lover or," as she's called herself, and they share a smile, an understanding that's grown from Lena's persistent question: "Am I just your lover, or . . . ?" an understanding that suits them quite well, as Lena, on a good day, thinks that the humorous twist is to her advantage, that she is *or*, in other words that she is *more* than a lover to him. Frans doesn't see any point in denying this, as things work well as they are, even though he doesn't really know what they are and what's going on, he knows practically nothing anymore, apart from the fact that he's now standing in the shower and thinking about the girl downstairs, and is *she* the one you think about when you stand masturbating in the shower, Lena has been known to ask, and if she's the one you think about then, if it's her you want, well, no, you don't need to answer, I know that's the truth, don't even *try* to deny it, no, don't touch me, go away, I don't want to see you, OUT! And this is followed by a long monologue from Frans, who is standing on the other side of the locked bathroom door, reassuring Lena (who is standing inside the bathroom looking at her small breasts in the mirror and sobbing quite loudly, and thinking it's always like this, *always*! And *when* is she ever going to experience anything else, to be loved, for example, when is she going to be loved, she never will be, never) that he never thinks of anyone other than her, that it doesn't work like that for him, it might do for others, but not for him, that he thinks about Lena all the time, when he's masturbating and when he's not masturbating, and at that point, Lena says: DO YOU? Because her heart sparkles at the thought that he thinks about her even when he's *not* masturbating, that she's more than a sex object and a lover, that she really means something to him, and Frans says, in a slightly muted way, "Yes," which makes Lena melt completely and open the door.

Frans showers with the young girl from downstairs in his mind's eye: she's standing with her back to him when he goes into the laundry in the basement, carrying a basket of washing, she's leaning over, pulling the wet clothes out of the washing machine, and she's wearing a very short dress and Frans suspects she's not wearing any panties underneath, but he can't be sure, because it's quite dim in the cellar, all he can see is a shadow and then she turns toward him with hooded eyes and tugs at her dress. Through the rush of the shower, he hears the phone ring, but he can't face answering, suddenly he can't face anything, he stands completely still until the phone stops ringing, then he gets out of the shower, dries himself with a towel that smells of perfume. The telephone starts to ring again and Frans sees on the display that it's Lena calling from work, as she always does, in case he's managed to find someone to be unfaithful with in the time it takes for her to get to work, take the elevator up to the fourth floor, walk along the corridor with a thumping heart and into the office to pick up the receiver, dial the number, and normally he answers, so he can be left in peace, he knows that she's calling to see what he's doing, whether for example he's fucking the girl from downstairs, I'm eating, he says, I was still asleep, he says, yes, it is nice weather, but today he says nothing, he doesn't answer the phone, and he realizes that it might be fatal, not to answer, and yet he doesn't, it rings and rings, but he doesn't answer. The ringing stops. He picks up the phone, records a new message on the answering machine: "Hi, it's Frans. I'm afraid I can't answer the phone right now, as I'm in the basement fucking the girl from downstairs up against a washing machine, but if you leave a message after the tone, I'll get back to you as soon as I've shot my load." Then he stands for a long time looking at the phone, with his heart pounding, until he finally grabs the receiver and changes the message back to the old one.

—

Frans goes into the kitchen and makes a cup of coffee, he sits with his head in his hands over the coffee that steams up into his face, but he can't be bothered to move it, he thinks about Lena, sits there for a long time pondering. He doesn't know if it's worth it, he misses his brother, sighs heavily when he realizes for the first time, for real, that his relationship with his brother has shrunk to that one look every morning after the bag of dog shit has been thrown onto Frans Ekman's balcony, and all because of Lena, who was Frans Ekman's brother's girlfriend a year ago. Frans suddenly has problems breathing, he stands up, goes into the living room, opens the balcony door, tries to breathe, and then lies down on the sofa and thinks what a crap day it is. And he thinks about Lena, that he should perhaps have said with more feeling that she suited the color of her new purple suit, when she stood there, ready for work, sashaying back and forth in front of him so he could see her from every angle, as he lay in bed and couldn't face getting up. He should have said that it suited her, because it really did, she actually looked sexy in it, but then something possessed him to say in answer to her "No, you don't really mean that," that she was right, that he thought, if he was going to be honest, that it was a terrible color that made her look as old as she was. Whereupon she marched out and slammed the door, determined not to call him all day, as punishment, until he said something to make it all right again.

—

And now Lena's coming up the stairs. But Frans can't hear her, he can't hear anything, he's sleeping off his misery. Lena comes up the stairs, only this time, again, with a gun, she has a gun in her bag, and she's standing in front of the door, rummaging around for her keys, she feels frozen inside, she sees what's waiting for her, she knows what's waiting for her, splayed legs are waiting for her, blonde hair, Frans's ecstatic face, she is frozen inside as though she were cold, but she's not shivering, she holds the gun in her hand in her bag and walks slowly into Frans's flat, into the living room, where Frans is lying stretched out. She stops, looks at him, moves closer to study his face for signs of what she knows was happening on the sofa before she came in, she moves closer, listens to his breathing, deep in and deep out, his mouth is open, and he's drooling onto the cushion, she sees that his hair is wet and as she stands there with the gun in her hand in her bag listening to his breathing, the drumroll reaches a crescendo, she feels a pain in her chest, or her back, which might at first be mistaken for affection, affection for the sleeping, innocent Frans, but which is in fact Frans Ekman's brother's knife, Frans Ekman's brother is standing behind her and has stabbed her in the back, he thinks it's about time that he showed them, got them back for all the pain they've caused him.

—

Good people, but still not able to get things right.

Blanchot Slips Under a Bridge

This is the story of how Maurice Blanchot slips under a bridge one day.

—

Maurice Blanchot woke up one morning with Arvo Pärt playing in his ears, without being able to explain why. He looked up at the ceiling and heard the piano notes in his head, loud and clear. At the same time, he saw a bridge in Prague, and he saw the wide gray river that flowed under the bridge, and the blackbirds that flocked and circled dramatically above. And in the middle of the bridge: nothing. Everywhere on the bridge: nothing. He couldn't remember having ever seen the bridge, nor having dreamed about it. It was suddenly just there in his mind's eye, when he woke up, with the music he could not remember having heard, or dreamed. His head was full of something completely new.

—

Maurice Blanchot got out of bed and went into the living room. His living room was empty. The wooden floor was cold under his bare feet and he thought to himself that it was definitely autumn. The room was cold and he looked out onto the street; the tree that reached up to his window had turned yellow without him noticing. He opened the window, stretched out, grabbed hold of a branch and shook it as hard as he could.

—

Voilà.

—

Yellow leaves rained down from the tree, spinning to the ground. He looked down. There were plenty there from before. It's definitely autumn! Blanchot said and shivered, as he was standing there in only his underpants. It smelled of damp soil. Rain. He closed the window. Went out into the hall to get his bag and pulled out the Arvo Pärt CD. The strange thing was that Blanchot had bought the CD the day before on his way home from a lonely evening in a lonely bar. He knew nothing about Arvo Pärt, he had just decided

ιp again. No, he *had* to jump. He took a
ɔ the quay, but then suddenly thought
be best to take off his thermal overalls,
dn't fill with water and pull Geir to the
ell. If only his hands weren't shaking so
it was bitingly cold. He peeled off the
pulled off the legs, took off his shoes,
there in his long johns, his woolen under-
brand-new, that he'd got for Christmas.
around. He hadn't shouted for help yet, he
why, but he hadn't known for sure if Asle
s serious or not. It might just be some crazy
f he did shout for help, and it was just a
then people would think he was in on it.
t was too late to shout, now that he was
ere in his long johns. People would think it
ho needed help. To get dressed again! Geir
t the thought. Oh, but there was no time to
ad to get a move on and jump. But then his
would get wet! The worst thing Geir knew
ool. It itched like hell. So he took them off.
hem off and put them down on the ther-
lls. The thermal overalls would be all right
en he got out, he could dry himself with his
vest. So now he was standing there in his
t and briefs. His trapper's hat—what was he
do with that? Asle must have drowned by
vas going to be too late, there was no time to

on impulse to go into the music shop that was open
late, and suddenly found himself staring at the light
green CD cover with a name on it that appealed to
him, without him being able to explain why, ARVO
PÄRT—it often happened to Maurice Blanchot that a
name appealed to him. He thought about names as
great, heavy freighters that glided past in the dark on
the world's vast oceans, never meeting, other than in
collision or by blowing their horns from a distance.
Buying the CD was like sounding his horn, a long call
from a lonely ship; he had bought it, put it in his bag.
Forgotten it. Gone to bed without thinking that he'd
bought a new CD. Fallen asleep. Woken with the music
playing in his ears. That is to say, how could he know
that it was that music he woke up to, playing in his
ears? He just knew that it was. He put the CD into the
CD player. Pressed play.

Voilà.

The music.

Precisely the music he had woken up to playing in
his ears. "How can you explain that?" Blanchot asked
no one. But the room was somehow full of something
completely new. Blanchot lay down on the bright blue
Persian carpet and listened. "It's like being underwater," he said. He closed his eyes, let his hands run
gently along the soft fibers of the carpet. The picture
of the bridge in Prague popped into his mind again.
But this time he was floating in the gray flowing water,

approaching the bridge feetfirst, he could see the toes of his shoes sticking up in front of him like the prow of a gondola, and the bridge was getting closer, like a mouth, closer and closer, the whole horizon was getting strangely close, a jagged city skyline, church spires, overhead tram lines, and the bridge. The bridge reared up dramatically above him and he slipped under, it got darker, he could only just make out the pattern of the cement that joined the stone blocks and then he slipped out on the other side, and he saw that in the time that he was under the bridge, dusk had fallen and a flock of blackbirds swooped over him. And then he spotted the soles of another pair of shoes. Coming in the opposite direction, upstream, toward the bridge. Blanchot lifted his head a little so that he could see better, and now he could see that the soles belonged to a long pair of legs, a body, and a head. It was I, Julio Cortàzar, who was floating toward him with the same surprised look on my face. As we slipped by one another, Maurice Blanchot said: "You're going against the current!" And I had time to say "No" before we passed one another, Maurice Blanchot going downstream, and I upstream and under the bridge.

Air

Geir stood on a spot of c[...] of ice, just where the rot[...] see anything of Asle, wh[...] Had he been holding the [...] jumped? Geir thought he h[...] and he couldn't see any [...] long as he hadn't tied hims[...] that, about people who wa[...] who tied themselves to a [...] loose or rise up again, in o[...] lessly to the bottom, and so[...] the bar of chocolate in his [...] it were burning, why on ea[...] chocolate with him? He wa[...] but then thought there was n[...] do something, maybe he sh[...] really didn't want to do that!)[...] toward the bar of chocolate,[...] doing, straightened up again. A[...]

straightened [...] step out on[...] that it woul[...] so they wou[...] bottom as [...] much! And [...] upper part [...] socks, stoo[...] wear, blue,[...] He looked [...] didn't kno[...] jumping w[...] idea. And [...] crazy idea[...] And now [...] standing t[...] was him [...] chuckled [...] lose. He l[...] long john[...] was wet [...] He took [...] mal over[...] there. W[...] thermal [...] string ve[...] going tc[...] now, he [...]

waste! He'd better keep it on. But then he'd—damn, he threw it down. He took some steps onto the quay. He was shivering. It was cold, and it was icy, and he was scared. The quay creaked. He should just run across before it collapsed! It would be a bit of a mess if the whole quay suddenly lay there floating on the surface, he might miss Asle in all the chaos, he made up his mind, felt it like a spasm in his stomach, he ran over and just then a head popped out of the water, a face drained of any color, a thin head gasping for air, and Geir slipped on a clump of ice, his legs shot into the air, and he knew with every fiber of his body, floating, that this was it, the quay was going to collapse, he was going to fall, and everything would be chaos. He landed heavily on his back, his back thumped down on the quay. The quay held. Dazed, he crawled back onto the asphalt. Asle scrambled to get ashore, he slipped on the stones. Geir limped over to him, bent down, held out his hand. Asle grabbed it, his hand was icy cold. Then he staggered onto dry land, white as a sheet and dripping. "I couldn't breathe," he said. "No," Geir said. "Just didn't work!" he said. "Sorry to hear that," Geir said. There was silence, Asle stood there dripping, gasping for air. "I've heard that you have to tie yourself to the stone," Geir said. "Or rather, I've read." Asle raised his eyebrows. "Right," he said. Geir nodded, a little uncertain. "Well, well," Geir said. "Quite a day! People have been slipping and falling outside the flower shop, I think there's a really icy patch there. Three in a row went down on their asses just now!" Asle nodded, looked around. Looked at Geir. And then walked off.

—

Geir stood there for a moment or two, watched him go, leaving behind a stream of seawater, his thin body giving off steam in the cold. Kipper, Geir thought, and had to laugh, his teeth were chattering because he was so cold, thin as a kipper. Then he felt the pain in the soles of his feet, he was standing on ice, it bit into his skin. His tailbone, his back ached. He limped over to the small pile of clothes. Looked around, put on his thermals. As he pulled his long johns up over his thighs, he saw Åsta toddling along pulling her cart behind her. She gave Geir a stern look, which he pretended not to see. He smiled, lifted his hand in greeting, and pulled his long johns up around his waist with the other hand. Pulled on his thermal overalls, his socks, shoes, and trapper's hat. Limped over to the van. His feet were cold, his stomach burning. Opened the door, got in, it hurt to sit down. Damn, he'd forgotten the bar of chocolate. But he didn't want to go back and get it now. Now that he was back in the van. But it was a whole bar of cooking chocolate! He didn't want to. But he opened the door carefully, all the same, stuck his foot out, but then heard someone coming, so he pulled it back in, closed the door. Too gently. Aargh! He opened the door wide, slammed it shut. He had to laugh. It must have looked odd! A van door being opened only to be slammed shut. He looked out at the street. Not many people about, all in all, no, must be the slippery ice. What about the houses, were people standing in the windows? He leaned forward and looked up at the houses. He saw a shadow move back from the window above the shoemaker. Geir swallowed. Turned on the radio. Too bad about the chocolate. He looked over at Åsta making her way over the ice with grips on her shoes. She waddled like a goose, Geir thought to himself. Goosta, he thought, and had to laugh, hehe, but it wasn't a proper laugh. Well, well, what a day it had been. He looked up at the window to see if there were any more people. He felt a warm flush through his body. He had been standing there in his underpants and vest. Phew, a bit hot in here! What should he do now, maybe he should just drive home, yes, maybe. Or he could sit here. People might think he'd left early because he was embarrassed. He wasn't embarrassed! And there might still be some entertainment to be had outside the flower shop, unless someone had salted the sidewalk. And then there was that bar of chocolate! He couldn't just drive off and leave it. No, he'd stay put.

Transcend

SHE *(doesn't really want this)*

SHE *(is fed up with herself and the situation)*

THIS SITUATION *(where she feels naked, undressed, FAR TOO MUCH longing, she wants it to stop, that is, at least, after THIS SITUATION, she wants it to stop)*

SHE *(believes that as a thinking person it should be perfectly clear that she is dealing with a Don Juan, but for a person of longing, it's not so easy)*

DON JUAN *("pron. don hwan; Span. 'Sir John,' a legendary libertine, womanizer, seducer, Casanova," is pulling off her sweater)*

SHE *(longs for the total fusion between two people and is bitterly aware that this is not possible with a Don Juan; he will just move on. A Don Juan is an absurd person, someone who exhausts all possibilities and moves on, who acts as though there were no consequences, as though there were no forever)*

SOME *(humanism, that is!!)*

SHE *(needs to imagine forever)*

SHE *(thinks of the world as an eternity where the total fusion is forever—a tautology in itself)*

ONE COULD CALL IT *(in principle, a longing, if you imagine that LONGING, as a feeling, stretches beyond its own boundaries, and so, if you pursue it, is a feeling that belongs to something eternal, in contrast to, say, happiness, which is transient and of a more instant nature)*

SHE *(gets more and more PISSED at the thought that once again she is distorting her own ideas in this situation)*

SHE *(wants a final and absolute end to this)*

SHE *(has thought of demonstrating this by not having an orgasm)*

HE *(is pulling off her sweater)*

HE *(is pulling off her pants and underwear)*

SHE *(makes some resistance)*

SHE *(stands there naked and undressed)*

HE *(does things with her nipples)*

HE *(does more things with her nipples)*

HE *(does things he knows she loves with her nipples)*

SHE *(loves what he's doing with her nipples)*

SHE *(hates him because he's doing things with her nipples that she loves)*

SHE *(has to lean against the wall)*

SHE *(has to close her eyes)*

SHE *(has to touch his hair)*

HIS HAIR *(is so soft)*

HE *(kisses her on the neck)*

SHE *(becomes a weak-willed wretch)*

SHE *(a weak-willed wretch, pulls down his trousers)*

SHE *(a weak-willed wretch, wants him on the spot)*

HE *(puts the weak-willed wretch's knees over his shoulders)*

SHE *(stretches her arms out)*

HE *(lowers his head)*

SHE *(lifts her head)*

HE AND SHE *(do it, with their heads just touching)*

SHE

HE

HEH

SHHE

SHH

EHH

HEH

EHE

EES

SHHE

SHE *(has an orgasm totally against her will)*

HE *(waits until she's stopped quaking)*

HE *(flips her over onto her stomach)*

OUTSIDE *(rain and sirens in an almost besotted confusion)*

RAIN AND SIRENS: ssshhh neenawneenaw sssshhhh neenawneenaw sssssshhhhhhhneenaneenaw-ssssshhhhh neenawneenaw

AS *(a parallel with what we have just been through)*

AS *(in another universe where the total fusion between two elements can be achieved)*

WHICH *(is in fact in this universe)*

IN PRINCIPLE *(too longed-for and fantastic to be true)*

BUT *(still)*

Meanwhile, on Another Planet

DIX24 is sitting at the kitchen table when PUZ32 slides into the room. DIX24 is so beautiful you could die, thinks PUZ32, how, she thinks, hiding her head in her hands, can one hurt something or someone so beautiful as much as she has to do? DIX24 looks at her astonished, then a Polaroid picture slips out of his head, he takes it out and hands it to her, it's a picture of PUZ32 as she is standing now, with her hands around her head. Then he pulls out another picture, which is blank, but with this symbol: "?" PUZ32 shakes her head. Then she pulls out a photograph. It is of PUZ32, naked, against the same kitchen table, with DIX27 behind her. DIX24 slides back from the chair while he stares at the photograph that slowly dissolves in front of his eyes. PUZ32's heart is hammering. Then she pulls out a picture of a small fetus. It's so beautiful. It's so small and the light around it is so red. It's sucking its thumb. It looks like it's dreaming. It's impossible to know about what. DIX24 closes his eyes, because it hurts! He is both furious and completely lost. He pulls a picture out of his head: DIX24 and PUZ32 eating hot dogs by a hot dog stand. PUZ32 opening her mouth around an enormous sausage with far too much onion. DIX24 is laughing. Another picture: DIX24 has won a pink teddy bear for PUZ32 and PUZ32 is hugging it. Another picture: DIX24 and PUZ32 walking hand in hand on the sand, the sun is setting and they are not wearing shoes. PUZ32's heart is about to break. She pulls out a picture that shows that her heart is about to break. But DIX24 doesn't see it. He's sitting with his eyes closed. He pulls out a picture that shows a water surface. He sits for a while. Then he pulls out another picture: a big bubble is about to break onto the surface of the water. PUZ32 throws herself at the picture in an attempt to dive into it, but too late, it dissolves, she shakes DIX24, but he has disappeared into himself.

—

What can we learn from this? That impossible situations can arise on other planets too. We don't need to think that we're the only ones who struggle and fight. Another striking feature is that they communicate through pictures.

Vitalie Meets an Officer

Oh, biographies! Anna Bae the Younger loved them. She loved the sentences in them. The way the sentences presented themselves as if what they said had actually happened. They were able to compress enormous timelines and state that it was like this or that, and that this is how this links to that. Right now she was reading a biography of the writer Arthur Rimbaud. She liked Rimbaud better than any other writer. Everything he said and did and wrote was rebellious! She would also dearly love to shout "fuck!" in the face of everything. She would also love to run away from home again and again.

—

She was sitting reading on a sofa that was green. She ran her hand over the fabric, it was an old sofa with a complicated pattern of flowers and leaves, and the flowers and leaves were in raised shiny velvet. It was uneven, and it felt good to run her hand over it. She, Anna Bae, was the third leaf, she thought as she sat there on the sofa and stroked her hand over the fabric, and looked at her hand, it was almost identical to her mother's hand, and as far as she could remember, that was almost identical with her mother's mother's hand. It was as if this hand lived its own life, it had moved down through the generations so it could continue to stroke the uneven, good-to-touch velvet on the sofa. As she stroked with her hand, which she no longer felt was a part of her, but felt more and more like some strange creature that was rubbing up against the velvet, against the sofa, she read about Rimbaud's mother, who was called Vitalie: "Although Vitalie's social life was confined to the church, shopping, and occasional games of whist, she somehow managed to meet a French army officer in 1852," and she threw herself back in delight:

—

SOMEHOW SHE MANAGED IT!

—

Sometimes when you read, it's like certain sentences strike home and knock you flat. It's as if they say everything you have tried to say, or tried to do, or everything you are. As a rule, what you are is one simmering, endless longing. And that was how this sentence struck Anna Bae's consciousness, like a quivering arrow of truth. That said: it's possible. To meet a French army officer. Or simply to manage whatever it is you are longing for. That seems impossible to manage. That blankets you like destiny. It would seem that Anna Bae's destiny was to be the third leaf, Anna Bae who was sitting on the same old sofa, stroking the hand that no one had managed to dispense with over the sofa that had been there for three generations. Her destiny was to be here, to live in this house, to walk in the fields outside the house, to gather the sheep from the mountain, never to go deeper into civilization than the hill down to the shop, and certainly never to talk to anyone other than the two neighbors who lived on the farms closest by. To buy books on the Internet. Her destiny was to be filled with a simmering, endless longing. That was her destiny, unfortunately! But Vitalie managed, all the same. One might wonder how. Anna had to ponder how, because of the way it was written, and nothing more was said. In one way or another, she had managed (this confined soul) to meet an officer. In 1852. She had just read that Vitalie Cuif, from the age of five, had been a mother to her two brothers and wife to her suddenly widowed father, that she sacrificed everything for the family until the age of twenty-seven, by which time she had become a bony, prim woman with scraped-back hair. Not a particularly promising starting point for meeting someone. But then she met this officer, somehow. And as a result, she gave birth to Arthur Rimbaud. Before the officer left the family when Arthur was six. Scraped-back hair! Anna, twenty-six, loosened her hair, which was pulled back into a ponytail, leaned back on the green sofa and, while stroking her hand over the uneven, good-to-touch pattern, came to the conclusion that the meeting between Vitalie and the officer could only have happened in the following way:

—

Her starting point was Nick Cave's song "(Are You) The One That I've Been Waiting For," where he sings, among other things: "I knew you'd find me, 'cause I longed you here." So, if one was to believe Cave, it was possible to long someone to you. One could imagine that Vitalie's longing lay like a well-hidden egg in her chest and purred unseen with glorious, secret dreams. And inside the egg lay her longing, which was not going to transform into a bird. No, it was shiny and thin, like a fishing line. The line lay coiled in Vitalie's chest and grew and grew like a baby bird until one day, one day she was lying on the bed, staring up at the ceiling and listening to her father tramping around in the next room—she was so fed up with that tramping! She couldn't bear that tramping anymore!—it started to tap on the shell that was inside her chest. The line tapped and tapped until it managed to break a hole in the shell, and then it wound out and through her chest, found its way through her ribs and out through her skin, and then it started to move about the room, in slow, undulating movements. Then it found a window, bored its way through the window frame and glass out into the air. Then it carried on down the road in the same slow, swinging movements. And anyone with extremely good hearing might have heard it buzzing, or humming, through the air. The line swung and looped around the town until it found an officer that took it by surprise. Something felt right about this officer. This officer was the one it had to be! The line pierced through his uniform, through his skin, found its way in through his ribs and wrapped itself around his heart. The officer felt an inexplicable pull. He was pulled through the town, his legs just walked and walked, until he finally found himself standing outside a window. There was an alluring light in the window, it was a dark winter's night outside, and there was a warm light in the window. He made a snowball, threw it at the window. Who was in there? A young woman. She stood there with her arms hanging by her side, and then she opened the window. She was very beautiful! Nothing prim about her, no scraped-back hair. Her hair was loose and her cheeks were flushed.

—

Anna didn't know if they had windows that could be opened in 1852; in fact, she wasn't sure if they had windows at all. She thought they had windows. She got up from the sofa and looked out at the vast fields around her. They were yellow, covered in a sharp layer of frost. Farther down, the fjord came into the bay, lay in it, held it tight. Later in the evening, she would stand here and watch the trailers creeping up the mountainside like moving constellations. Anna went over to another window, looked up toward the road, the streetlights were just coming on, emitting a pale halo. The forest was black. She went into the kitchen and looked out the window. The fjord, the forest. She let down her hair. She took a knife and carved her name into the kitchen table, and the year: "Anna Bae, 2004." Now she was ready. She ran her finger over the letters on the table, and just knew it. Everything was buzzing. She was warm and happy.

—

Then she heard a low sound, a kind of humming, in the air. She looked out and to her great surprise saw a UFO landing on the field over there. It was shaped like two soup dishes glued together with a row of flashing lights around the middle. Anna stood there staring and waiting to see if a door would open, if a ladder would drop down. But nothing happened. It was as though it was waiting. Who are they waiting for? Anna thought as she pulled on her boots and jacket. Is it me? she wondered as she walked over the frozen grass that crunched under her boots. It wasn't a big UFO, she could see that, smaller than she had imagined UFOs to be. And it wasn't silver, as she thought they were, but dark. Dark. And—she refused to believe it. She walked right up to it and put her hand on the UFO wall. It was covered in a green fabric, just like the one on her sofa. Exactly the same. The UFO was covered in green velvet in a complicated pattern of flowers and leaves. Some of the flowers and leaves were in raised, shiny velvet, and it was uneven and it felt good to stroke your hand over it. It was the strangest thing Anna Bae had ever experienced. To stand there and stroke and pat a UFO.

The Object Assumes an Exalted Place in the Discourse

Here is the object: it's shaped like a polygonal prism and is luminous green. Can everyone picture it? Okay. This object comes *sailing* into the discourse, which we can think of as darkness. As if the object came sailing in through space. Slowly. The music we hear in the background is the music from *Blade Runner*, and the sound of the small flying cars that Harrison Ford uses. The object now sails slowly ahead, before starting to climb up and up, until it docks some way up in the discourse. And it sits there glowing. Yes, in an elevated position, just as Roland Barthes describes it in *Writing Degree Zero*. We let the magnifying glass glide over Barthes's text, and see the word "discontinuous." We carefully study a sentence we love: "The interrupted flow of the new poetic language initiates a discontinuous nature, which is only revealed piecemeal. At the very moment when the withdrawal of functions obscures the relations exist-ing in the world, the object in discourse assumes an exalted place." It is absolutely no surprise that at this point we have the picture of a luminous green prism sailing in through the dark and taking an exalted place on our retina, a bit like when you've been staring too hard at a lamp on the ceiling and then close your eyes! How strange, we think, that a sentence that was written to explain an aspect of modern poetry can have roughly the same effect on our imagination as science fiction. In particular, the phrase A DISCONTINUOUS NATURE, WHICH IS ONLY REVEALED PIECEMEAL makes us imagine a vast darkness and then rectangular blocks of bright green sections of nature, and they are not lined up as such, but appear in flashes. The blocks of bright green and sudden nature appear in flashes. And when the light disappears, they vanish into the dark like spooky, withdrawing creatures. And the phrase AT THE VERY MOMENT WHEN THE WITHDRAWAL OF FUNCTIONS OBSCURES THE RELATIONS EXIST-ING IN THE WORLD makes us picture "functions" as the switches in a spaceship that has lost contact with the Earth, which has been visible down there as a bluish-white marble until now, but now it's gone, all is dark, and THE OBJECT IN DISCOURSE ASSUMES AN EXALTED PLACE. A bit like a ballet, where the plot involves nothing more than a ballet dancer suddenly entering the stage, then standing there completely still. Or a small plot in a short text that can be summarized in as many words as the text itself: "The object assumes an exalted place in the discourse."

Two by Two

At ten minutes to one, one night in November, Edel loses it. She has been standing by the window with her arms crossed since ten past twelve, alternately looking down the drive and then at the watch on her wrist. Sometime before this, she lay on the bed clutching a book to her chest with her eyes shut tight and felt good, strong, and completely open. Then she got up to clear the snow, so that Alvin could drive straight into the garage without having to stop and clear the snow himself first. She wanted to *reach out* to him—that was the expression she used when she thought about what it was she wanted to do; it was a cliché, but that was okay, it was what she wanted. She imagined her own small hand reaching out and being taken by Alvin's hand, Alvin's big, strong hand. Her eyes filled with tears when she thought of their two joined hands and everything they symbolized. And clearing the snow—it dawned on her that clearing the snow symbolized that she was making room for him again. She

was making room for him again after he had asked for
forgiveness and said that from now on, she was the
only one, there would be no others; she had let him
stay in her life as Thomas's father, as someone she
shared her home with, someone she refused to look in
the eye at the breakfast table and whose shoes she
occasionally kicked as she passed them in the hallway.
She shoveled and cleared the snow and as she shoveled, she looked up at the double garage and thought
that it symbolized her goal, she was clearing the way
for him—she was the garage that he could come home
to. Her small car was already parked on one side of the
garage and when his car was on the other side, things
would be as they should be. Her small car parked
alongside his big car. She ran up to the garage through
the uncleared snow and turned on the light and looked
at her little car that was standing there all alone, waiting, and she cried as she cleared the rest of the driveway to the garage.

—

That was forty minutes ago. And it's snowing hard
again now, snowing so much that it looks like the snow-
flakes are falling together, two by two, three by three,
four by four, falling through the air until they land
suddenly and mutely in the snow. In only forty minutes,
the driveway has been covered again. And the man

she cleared the way and made room for is not here and the fact that things are *not* as they should be screams out at Edel. He should have been here forty minutes ago. The last ferry docked at twenty past eleven and it takes three quarters of an hour to drive here from the ferry—and that's being generous. In other words, he should have been here at ten past twelve, when she finished clearing the snow and stood waiting, red-cheeked, by the window with a magnanimous, nearly loved-up look on her face. Every minute that passed after ten past twelve pulled this look of love from her, like a net being dragged from the water, and by the thirtieth minute past twelve, when she called his mobile and heard it ringing in the breadbox in the kitchen, her face was no longer remotely magnanimous. She screamed with rage, she, who had felt no rage one hour earlier as she lay on the bed feeling good, strong, and open and then decided to get up so she could clear the snow. At that point, in the thirtieth minute past twelve, there was nothing left in the body with the crossed arms that was in any way still touched by the good, light magnanimity she had felt blossom in her heart just over an hour ago, as she lay on the bed and read *Birthday Letters* by Ted Hughes. The English poet Ted Hughes wrote the book for his deceased wife, Sylvia Plath (also a poet). In the book he expresses his love for Sylvia, who took her own life largely because she felt that this love was lacking—

she believed that he did not love her, that he was unfaithful, which he was, and on February 11, 1963, she put her head in a gas oven and took her own life. And in the years that have followed, the English press and many others have held Ted Hughes responsible and criticized him for not talking about it, for not expressing any regret, or even asking for forgiveness, nothing. He has received prizes for his poetry, but people look at him with eyes that no doubt clearly express what they really think of his behavior. Edel is one of those who have held it against him. She loved Sylvia Plath and she has borne a grudge against Ted Hughes. Though she has found some solace in the fact that even among famous poets there are those who share her experience. She, as a small bookseller in a rural community, can recognize herself in a famous poet, Plath—there *are* bonds between people, she thought; even successful poets in big cities wander around in their own homes in desperation, even they rage and throw things against the wall. The fact that they cried and felt small, small and betrayed, that they wanted to be stones that would sink to the bottom and stay there, was a huge relief to her. It was awful that Sylvia had suspected Ted and was right. Because that meant it was possible: to suspect and to be right.

But then she read *Birthday Letters*. With great resentment, she picked the book with the red poppies on the cover from the cardboard box of books that she had ordered and with great reluctance she opened the book and read the first poem. She didn't know how it happened, but as she read the book, it struck her: even though he betrayed her, he must have loved her, he *saw* her, saw all the big and small things that she went around doing and feeling—and if only she had known *that*, Sylvia, as she went around doing all those things that she did not think were noticed! When she got to the last poem, she discovered that the red poppies on the cover referred to this poem about the red poppies that Sylvia had loved and seen as a symbol of life; and this evening, as she, Edel, lay on the bed reading this last poem, she felt she was the one who saw all this for her, in a stream of warmth and the dark timbre of the voice that *saw* and *said*, that twisted and twisted down and down until finally she could barely breathe, suffocated by a pressing joy, or sadness: This Is Life, You Are Loved and You Are Betrayed in That, That Is Life, I Must Accept It, I Accept It: Life Is Good, Painful, and *Awful*! She thought to herself: This is *Acceptance*! The notion of "acceptance" radiated inside her like the sun suddenly staring through the clouds, forcing them open and covering the fjord like an iridescent bridal veil. This is *God*, thought Edel, and she felt like she was about to explode; she clutched the book to her breast and closed her eyes and felt completely open. She also felt overwhelmed by something else and had to scribble down some words on a piece of paper: "the power of literature."

—

The reason that Edel let go of this good, magnanimous feeling, of the notion of "acceptance," and has now lost the plot instead, is that she cannot see, but suspects, the scene that was unfolding in a house by the ferry around the same time that she was clearing the snow from the driveway, a forty-five-minute drive from the double garage at the end of the driveway. The scene that Edel suspected when she lost it, but could not see, looked like this: Her husband, Alvin, was standing behind Susanne, who lives in the house that stands alone by the ferry, a forty-five-minute drive from the double garage. They were both naked, Susanne was bending forward and holding on to a window ledge. Alvin was standing behind her and holding her hips. Alvin thought to himself that this was not what was supposed to happen, this was not what he had intended, he should have driven straight home, he should never have called in on Susanne, just to say hello, to find out if she was very sad because he had stopped coming, if she had been all right in the last six months, and to say that it was difficult, nearly impossible, just to drive by her house when he finished work, to say that he stood up on the bridge of the ferry and tried to see her inside every evening when she had the lights on and it was dark all around, and her house twinkled at him like a small star in the night sky, but that it couldn't carry on, he had a family to consider, Edel had threatened to leave him and take Thomas with her and he couldn't bear that, he had to sacrifice their love for Thomas, that was the way it was, that was what he wanted to say, he wanted to take responsibility for his family, that was what he had chosen, having spent a long and painful period thinking and doubting, he couldn't come in and stand here like he was now, holding her by the hips and pressing his cock between her legs.

—

Thomas—for whom Alvin was going to sacrifice his love and not stand as he is standing now, for his sake—is asleep. He has been out all afternoon selling raffle tickets in the snow and spent the whole time thinking about Noah's ark, which he learned about at school. He thought about giraffes and leopards. He thought about rhinoceroses and dreamed of stroking them and sitting on their backs, touching their horns. He thought about how enormous the boat must have been, as the teacher said yes when he asked if it was bigger than the hotel. He wondered whether there were also two ants on board. And two lice! And now he was lying curled up like a small fetus, dreaming about crocodiles. Because there were crocodiles on board, he had asked about that. He is dreaming about a big crocodile that has laid a crocodile egg in a nest, while Edel storms through the sitting room and pounds up the stairs to the bedroom. She throws on a pair of pants and a sweater, puts on a pair of shoes, and hurls *Birthday Letters* at the wall as hard as she can. Alvin comes all over Susanne's buttocks. In the crocodile nest, the first baby crocodile breaks through the hard shell of the egg. A rhinoceros stands for a long time looking at another rhinoceros, then suddenly walks away, out of the ark's big front door, and the rhinoceros that is left behind doesn't know why. Thomas shouts to Noah: Wait! Wait for the other rhinoceros! He tugs at Noah's tunic. Then he runs toward the door to bring back the rhino that has walked away. The one that was left behind falls to the ground with a great thud.

―

Thomas stands in the doorway with tousled hair. "Something went bump, Mommy," he says. "It was a book I threw against the wall," replies Edel. "Why did you throw it against the wall?" asks Thomas. "I was angry," says Edel. "It was a bad book. A terrible, terrible book. Put your clothes on, Thomas, we have to go and get Daddy." "Why?" asks Thomas. "His car has broken down and he can't get home. Hurry up," she says, and Thomas says that he doesn't want to, he has to sleep! If he doesn't go to sleep now, the rhinoceros might leave forever! "You can dream in the car," Edel says. "But I might not dream the same thing!" says Thomas. "Of course you will. Come on, I'll help you get dressed," she says and takes him firmly by the arm, her whole body shaking. "I want to dream the same thing!" Thomas whines.

—

Susanne is shaking. She stammers. "Alvin," she says, and turns toward him, wanting him to put his arms around her. "I love you," she whispers into his neck. "I knew you'd come back." He holds her tight but says nothing. "I can't say it," he says finally. "You know I have said that I can't. It would be wrong. It would build up your hopes, you know I would love to . . . but Thomas . . ." She nods and looks at him, he can see that she is not entirely happy. But she tells herself that she can cope with anything and that he must be able to see that, on her face, how big and generous she is. Maybe that will make him understand that deep down, he loves her and that it would be impossible,

impossible to leave her. She looks at him with an under-standing expression on her face.

—

"Fucking hell, I have to clear the snow again," shouts Edel. "Fucking fuck, shit, *shit*!"

—

She drives through the village through the snowstorm, her windshield wipers racing furiously back and forth, and a triangle of snow builds up under one of them, in a while she will no doubt have to get out and brush it off. Triangle! Naturally, a symbolic triangle had to appear right in front of her very eyes! She snorts, Ted Hughes, she snorts, that she could be so stupid. Oh, *Life*—right. Oh, *Terrible*, Oh Good, Oh Pain, it is none of that, it is pure and simple lunacy and shit. And the outside is just bodies, skeletons packaged in flesh, doing this and that and nothing makes sense. That, thinks Edel, and laughs a sad laugh aloud for herself, is what I will say at the seminar on Monday. "Mooommmyyy," complains Thomas. She has woken him, he is lying across the backseat with his duvet over him. She let him lie down without putting the seat belt on. "Go to sleep," she says. She has been taking courses in English literature at the college in the next village and up until now has enjoyed the course "Symbolism in Literature." She felt that it was true that you shouldn't scorn symbolism and simply look at it as antiquated, romantic thought, things should make sense, the expression and the content, she believed that something could stand for something else, a rose for love, an ocean for life, a cross for death, but now it just irritates her, because now she realizes that of the two lanes on the road along the fjord toward the ferry, only her side has been cleared, she immediately thinks: *Is that how it is*, is that what this means, is his path closed, will he not come back, it is only she who can reach out to him, and he cannot reach her, is his lane full of snow, is that how it is? She feels helpless, is that what this means? No, she refuses to read it symbolically! It is just a road, she thinks, a stupid road, without any symbolic meaning. Crap and idiocy, and on top of that, asphalt. She wishes she had furry dice hanging from the mirror, or a Wunderbaum, the most pointless thing she can think of, when she gets back to the village, she will stop at the gas station and buy a Wunderbaum, to remind her of this, to mark this evening when she said goodbye to symbolic thinking and to—what, what else is she going to say goodbye to? Her marriage? But she is on her way to collect him, why, why is she doing it, should she rather drive back home and lock the door, let him sleep in the garage, should she stop driving, should she just stop, why did she react in this way, it had to be the least reflected-on thing she had ever done, she just did it, and what should she do now, should she carry on driving? She slows down as she swings into a wide bend, she sees an orange light pulsing in the trees on the other side of the road, it must be a snowplow, she is frightened of snowplows, she comes to a near standstill and lets the snowplow sail past on the far side of the road, the snow blasting over the barrier on the other side and hitting the trees and tears come to her eyes, spontaneously, *because now his lane is also being cleared.*

——

Alvin looks at Susanne's face, the pleading in her eyes makes him ashamed, he kisses her on the cheek and goes to look for his pants. "What have you been up to recently, then?" he asks, and Susanne tries to hold in her stomach as she picks up her bra from the floor. "Not much, same as always really . . . no, hang on . . ." She has thought of something. "Give me a second," she says, and with a sparkle in her eyes, she pulls on her panties and practically runs to the CD player. Alvin thinks suddenly there is something helpless about her body, dressed only in underwear, as she bends down to put on some music, he feels like he can't breathe, he tightens the belt on his pants and pulls on his jacket. "Susanne, I'm going to have to go. Edel will flip if

I'm not home soon, I'm sorry, Susanne," he says. But Susanne doesn't listen to him, she has put on a CD of salsa music and starts to dance in front of him. He must not go. She must get him to stay. She must get him to say something nice to her before he goes. "I've been going to salsa classes!" she says and dances closer and closer to him, with a provocative, slightly coy look. She takes him by the hands, he says, "Noooo . . ." then she lets go and turns her back to him as she rolls her hips. She's a bit nervous, so her dancing feels contrived. Alvin is so embarrassed on her behalf that he goes over to the dancing back and puts his arms around her and says that he really *must* go now, but that she's good at dancing, and she should carry on with it. "I'm a fool, Susanne," he says. "No, you're not," she says. "You are the best person I know." He kisses her on the forehead. "I might go to Cuba soon," she says, even though it's not true. "Well, I hope you have a good time then," he says.

—

Edel shakes her head, she does not want to think about it anymore, she does not want to interpret things symbolically anymore. We have rejected nature, that is what we have done, thinks Edel, as she drives slowly forward on the newly cleared road and the snowstorm gradually dies down, yes, nature has been abandoned

and we are to blame, we have focused on language
and become complicated. We have to get back to nature, we have to stop reading books, we have to stop
interpreting everything, we have to stop thinking fig-
uratively, we have to live like animals, we have to eat
food and sleep. We must renounce symbolism. We
must stop thinking altogether. We must live in one
simple dimension. Ah! She is happy. She feels mad. Or
perhaps she has actually been mad up to this moment and has now regained her sanity. She has a horrible, crystal-clear feeling in her head. As if her head
is two wide-open eyes with a cold wind blowing into
them. She shakes her head. Your husband has fucked
another woman this evening. She wants to laugh. And
so we have to stop thinking symbolism! Haha. Jesus!
she mumbles. And then laughs again. What a thing to
mumble. In fact, she wants to cry. She has to pull into
a bus stop and cry. Imagine, she thinks as she leans
forward over the steering wheel, crying. Imagine if it's
not what I think, but that he's been in an accident.
She looks over her shoulder at Thomas, he is sleeping,
lying with his face to the back of the seat, and she can
only see his hair sticking up from the duvet, a small
fan that spreads across the pillow and she thinks: then
he will be fatherless and she will be a single mother,
and she leans over the wheel again.

Alvin cannot quite understand what has happened. He drives home along the fjord, it has stopped snowing, the branches on the trees on the mountainside are weighed down, the road is white, no one has driven here since the snowplow, no tracks on the snow. The streetlights stand silently with bowed heads off into the distance, he imagines the noise that is made when the light from each streetlamp hits the roof of his car as he drives past, *bzzzzzzzzt*, he imagines that they are X-ray beams that penetrate the roof of the car and illuminate him, so that if you were looking in from the outside, you would see a skeleton sitting there holding the wheel and driving along the road. Out of the light: a man. In the light: a skeleton. On, off, on, off. In a kind of corny gray light, you can now see his right hand with all its white bones moving like tentacles, gripping the gear stick and shifting. And then he dresses the skeleton up in bluish-red muscles, veins, and sinews, just as he remembers from that picture in the anatomy book at secondary school that made a lasting impression on him: a person without skin, only muscles, veins, and sinews. Teeth without lips, eyeballs without eyelids. Sometimes it comes back to him, like when Edel was shouting and screaming and saying it was over, he could only just hear what she was saying, he stood there staring at her, he imagined her as a face without skin, only bluish-red, knotted muscles in her cheeks, over her lips and teeth. He feels hot, flushed,

conspicuously flushed, and it will not have died down
by the time he reaches home, he knows that, because
he has done it before, he should really take a long de-
tour when he gets to the village, but that won't be of
much help either, as then he will get home even later
and Edel will know, maybe she will have packed the
suitcase on wheels like she did the last time—the
good, big red suitcase on wheels—and then remembered that it was a gift from him and stopped right in
front of the front door, opened the suitcase and taken
out all the clothes, then kicked the suitcase across the
floor so that it hit the chest of drawers and lay there
open like a gaping mouth, just like the last time, and
then run up into the attic and searched and searched
until she found the old bag that was the bag she had
brought her clothes in when she moved in with him,
as she had the last time, to make a symbolic point to
herself that she was on her own again, and then woken
Thomas up and gone down to the hotel; maybe he
smells of perfume, he thinks, thank God he took
her from behind, touching as little skin as possible
from the waist up. It was really only the lower part
of his stomach that had touched her hips. He pictures Susanne's salsa-rolling hips and feels sick. He
stops the car, in the middle of the road, gets out of
the car, leaves the door open, walks to the edge of the
road, turns around, stretches his arms out from his
body, and allows himself to fall backward into the

snow. It is soft. If he lies here for a while, he will cool down. He will lie here and slowly but surely erase Susanne from his mind. Because now he can feel it in his bones, it is over.

—

Susanne pulls on some sweatpants and opens a bottle of wine, she sits down on the sofa and tries to think that she has just had a visit from her lover and that she is a grown woman with a rich life. She managed to get him to come. He could not stop thinking about her. He could not get her out of his mind—that's how strong the power is that she is fortunate enough to possess. But she knows there's no point. She tries not to think about the desperation that drove her to dance for him. She tries not to think about the embarrassed look on his face when she wanted him to dance. She drinks the glass of wine in one go, swallowing only a couple of times. It tastes of alcohol. Susanne purses her lips and goes over to the phone, looks up the number of a travel agent in the telephone directory. She just doesn't understand, she thinks, how Alvin, the best person she knows, who is so sensitive and observant, who has told her the strangest things about what he thinks, could just come like that and fuck her and then leave with an embarrassed, hard expression on his face. She feels it deep down, that he will not come back. It is over this time. She hopes he has an accident. She hopes he has an accident and ends up in the fjord. She dials the number for the travel agent. He could quite possibly have an accident with all this snow. The travel agency is closed and will open again tomorrow morning at 8:00 a.m., and she throws herself down on the floor. She wonders if she should slide her way over to the sofa, she lies on the floor and pictures herself wriggling exhausted and doomed like a soldier on a muddy battlefield, over to the sofa—but she knows that it's not true, the truth is that she is lying on her back on the floor, that she is looking up at the ceiling, that the back of her throat is burning and that the tears are running from her eyes down into her ears.

—

"*Please*," says Thomas. The missing rhino has not come back and Thomas is not allowed to leave the ark. Noah is so big that he nearly reaches the ceiling and he says firmly that it is not possible to go out, it has started to rain so they have to shut the door soon. Thomas tries to get to the door all the same, but the floor is heaving with baby crocodiles, so he slips and falls and never gets to the door. Now he notices that there is an elevator like the one in the hotel beside the door and he can see that it is on its way down, because the floor numbers are showing on a panel above the door, and he thinks that maybe it's the rhinoceros, 2, 1, *pling*: it's two lizards. The lizards clamber over to the baby crocodiles. Edel lifts her head from the wheel. She starts the car and swings out into the road. "Fucking shit," she mumbles.

Damn, fuck, shit, *shit*.

—

Alvin has made an angel in the snow, which he realizes is a great paradox, symbolically. It makes him think about Edel, which makes him want to cry, without managing to, he sits up, pulls up his knees, and sits huddled in his own angel. A pathetic, overly symbolic position, thinks Edel as she pulls up beside him before he has looked up. He looks up. He is not surprised to see her there. She stops the car, gets out, and stands in front of him. "What's happened?" she says. He shrugs his shoulders and opens his hands. Closes them again. "This," he says. "I made an angel in the snow." "You little shit," she says, and nearly starts to laugh, she is not reacting as she thought she would, she had imagined the scene and it was not like this, she shouted and cried and then he fell to the ground, but now it feels as if she is not here and the whole thing is slightly comical. "We're finished," she says, without feeling anything, and then goes back to sit in the car, her head feels crystal clear and cold, nearly light. Her feet feel light as well. "The car broke down!" he shouts, coming after her. "Fucking hell, Edel! I've been standing here for nearly an hour. And I couldn't phone you because I couldn't find my mobile! I've been sitting here waiting for help, but no one came." The crystal-clear, light Edel smiles. "I would have liked to see that," she says. Alvin says nothing, but gets into his car and his hands shake as he turns the key, because now it *is* over.

—

But the car does not start.

—

The car just manages to splutter a few times but does not start. "There you go," says Alvin. Edel says nothing. The blood is about to leave her legs and rush to her head, her cheeks. She looks at him, coughs. Nothing that is happening now is as she had imagined. She doesn't know whether this is true or not. "Get out of the way," she says and sits down in the driver's seat of his car, it is cold in the car. She turns the key, the car barely reacts. It is true. The car has broken down. She does not know what to do. She has driven along the fjord to collect him, to shout at him and leave him, or collect him, or leave him, and her side of the road was cleared of snow first, and then his side was cleared, it hits her, that actually happened. It literally happened. She goes around to the trunk and gets out a towrope and hands it to him. Alvin stands looking at Thomas, who is sleeping in the backseat, and tries to behave like someone whose car has broken down and who has been waiting in the snow for an hour. "What's he been up to today?" he asks, casually, and coughs. "He learned about Noah's ark and sold raffle tickets," Edel replies. "Come and look at him," Alvin says. Edel stands beside him and looks in at Thomas. He is lying with his arms stretched out above his head, up the back of the seat. In the same position that Susanne is now lying on the floor, without knowing that the painful pressure she feels in her heart is that same pressure that is in Edel's and Alvin's hearts right now, as they stand there side by side.

—

Edel drives the small car and tows the big car, which Alvin is steering. She refuses, she thinks, to interpret this symbolically. It's just the way things have turned out. They drive along the fjord. It's night. There are three of them. And the fact that there is a rope between the cars has no significance other than the physical fact that when a car breaks down it needs to be towed. I just don't understand this, thinks Alvin. He feels that he is being watched, as if someone is laughing at him; he said the car had broken down, and that is what happened. He got exactly what he asked for. He leans forward toward the windshield to see if he can see the stars, but is blinded by the light from the streetlamps, which stand silently with bowed heads, illuminating the cars as they pass. At regular intervals along the road, you can see a skeleton, an adult, sitting at the wheel, then a child's skeleton lying across the backseat, and then finally another adult skeleton, which is sitting more or less directly behind the first. The adult skeletons have their arms in front of them, holding the wheel, the child skeleton is not holding anything but has its arms stretched out above its head.

—

You can also see a larger skeleton, standing on all fours, which has a huge horn on its snout; it's standing beside the child skeleton. A similar skeleton now appears to the left, to the surprise of the first rhinoceros skeleton, because it lifts its head and looks expectantly at the approaching rhinoceros skeleton. They stand for a moment staring at each other and then the one rhinoceros rubs up against the other. A couple of antelope skeletons wander past and a tiger skeleton and a lion skeleton, and farther along, two small cat skeletons and then dogs and a mass of small crocodile jaws that nibble the child skeleton's legs, making it laugh and wriggle. And if X-rays could also show the contours and shape of other things that were not of solid, indisputable mass, you would be able to see the outline of an enormous wooden boat, with pairs of skeletons, two by two, on many levels, two for each sort of animal. A big human skeleton lifts its arms and then everyone feels what they are standing on leave the ground and float through the air.

Notes

"From the Lighthouse" is based on the book *Barn på fyr—minner om oppvekst* (Children at the lighthouse—memories of childhood) by Ragnhild Roald, Aschehoug, 2003.

"It's Snowing" quotes a poem by Gunnar Ekelöf, in the translator's own translation.

"Vitalie Meets an Officer" cites the biography *Somebody Else—Arthur Rimbaud in Africa, 1880–91*, by Charles Nicholl, Vintage, 1998.